# CLEANING UP IN THE VALKYRIE SUITE

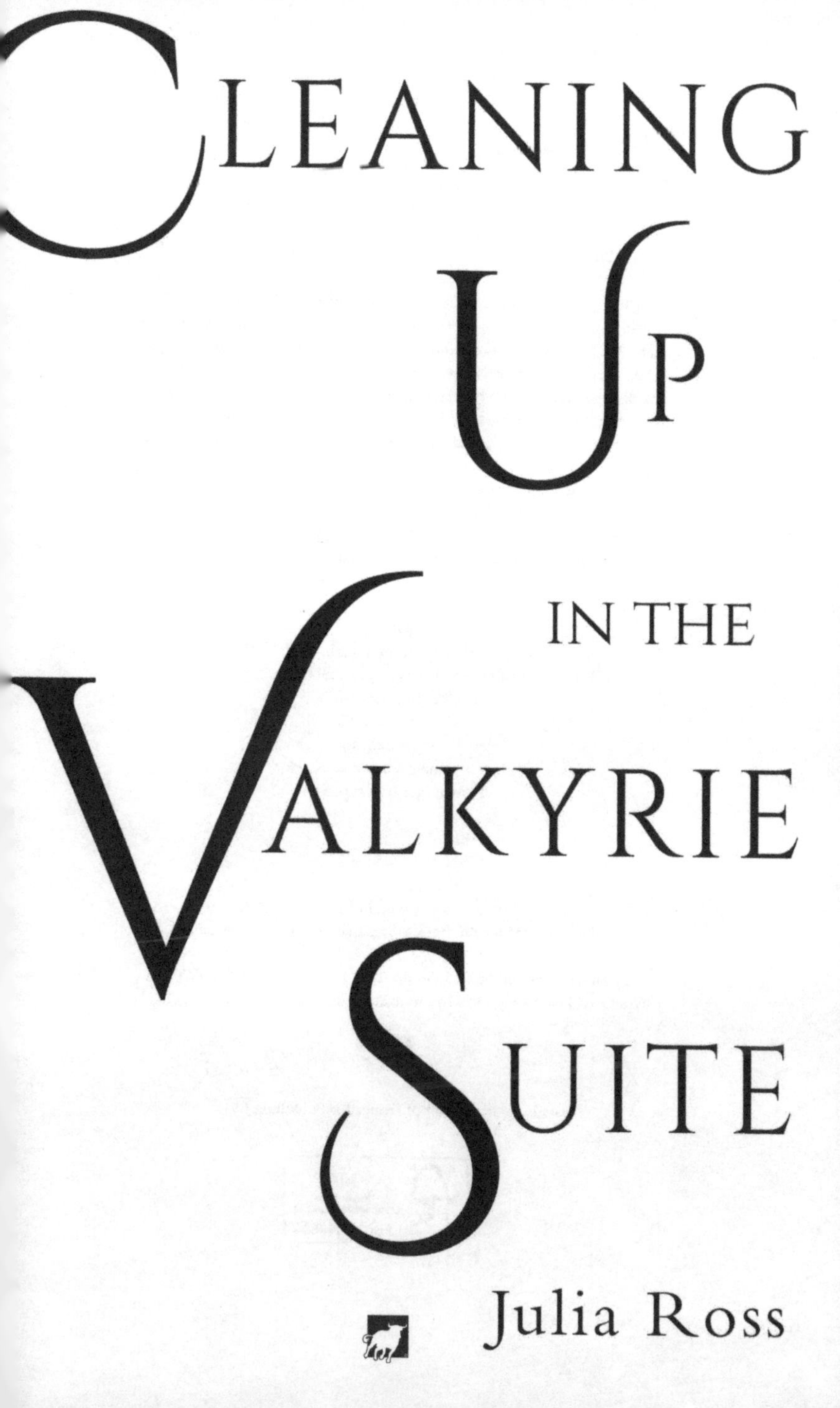

# Cleaning Up in the Valkyrie Suite

Julia Ross

Copyright © 2016 Julia Ross

The moral right of the author has been asserted.

Apart from any fair dealing for the purposes of research or private study, or criticism or review, as permitted under the Copyright, Designs and Patents Act 1988, this publication may only be reproduced, stored or transmitted, in any form or by any means, with the prior permission in writing of the publishers, or in the case of reprographic reproduction in accordance with the terms of licences issued by the Copyright Licensing Agency. Enquiries concerning reproduction outside those terms should be sent to the publishers.

This is a work of fiction. Names, characters, businesses, places, events and incidents are either the products of the author's imagination or used in a fictitious manner. Any resemblance to actual persons, living or dead, or actual events is purely coincidental.

Matador
9 Priory Business Park,
Wistow Road, Kibworth Beauchamp,
Leicestershire. LE8 0RX
Tel: 0116 279 2299
Email: books@troubador.co.uk
Web: www.troubador.co.uk/matador
Twitter: @matadorbooks

ISBN 978 1785892 370

British Library Cataloguing in Publication Data.
A catalogue record for this book is available from the British Library.

Printed and bound by CPI Group (UK) Ltd, Croydon, CR0 4YY
Typeset in 11pt Minion Pro by Troubador Publishing Ltd, Leicester, UK

Matador is an imprint of Troubador Publishing Ltd

# Chapter One

When it's windy, I find it almost impossible to sleep. It isn't the banshee howls or the tapping of leaves on windows that keeps me awake. My house is called 'The Tower' not 'Wuthering Heights' and there's no Heathcliff tap-dancing on the sill demanding to be let in. The reason for my insomnia is simply nervous anticipation. I'm listening for the sound of slates being ripped off the roof and smashed on the ground. I always thought a round shape was stronger architecturally than one with corners, but the tower roof has more patches in it than an Amish quilt, and still the tiles loosen and fall. I used to have my bedroom upstairs in the tower or 'the great stone phallus' as my fiancé, Conrad, called it. There's a short flight of stairs that leads to it from the upper landing.

My family moved into this large Edwardian villa, near Victoria Park and the university, when I was five and my brother ten. Geoffrey instantly staked his claim to the tower bedroom and my mother would have let him have it. 'No' didn't figure much in her exchanges with her son. But on this occasion, Dad spoke up:

"Geoffrey's a young idiot. He'll climb out of the window for a lark and kill himself. Prudence is much more sensible. We can trust her with the tower room as her bedroom."

“Why don’t you share it as a playroom?” my mother suggested. She knew perfectly well why not. Geoffrey shared nothing. He has never forgiven me for terminating his tenure as the only child of the family. He probably would have pushed me out of the window if we had been forced to share the room. But this was one of the few times that my father’s word prevailed, with the result that the round room, with its coloured glass roundels of pink and purple lilies in the window, became mine and stayed mine for the next forty years. It was a room that had leapt straight out of an illustration of the Lady of Shalott, and I’ve woven many a story in there over the years.

The room made me very popular throughout my school years. Girls who had seen my house, and girls who had only heard about it, were desperate to have an invitation to play in Rapunzel’s tower. Later on, at grammar school, sophisticated young ladies lost their cool at the thought of listening to ‘Pick of the Pops’ in my space capsule. When I lost that popularity, it became my refuge; my nun’s cell for my hours of devotion to working out how I’d messed up my life. Now, it’s beyond habitation. The last builder who went in there told me it was a death trap: the floor joists have rotted and need replacing. And then, on windy nights, another tile makes its bid for freedom and in comes more water. When I wove stories of my future in that room I fancied myself as the Lady of Shalott and I dared to leave it once for my failed brush with reality. But unlike the Lady, I didn’t die, just changed into another Tennyson heroine – Mariana in the Moated Grange, waiting. In my case, waiting for the whole bloody building to crash down around my ears.

Lots of people have told me that the house is too big for

one person, as if I, the one haunting the edifice, might not have noticed the fact. It's too expensive for me to heat, let alone repair. I can't even afford just to be in it because the council tax is in the highest band. I ought not to be here any more. I ought to leave the house before the last few pounds leave my account. I know all this.

When I was working at Grearson's, on a good salary, and when my mother was still alive, we had talked about remortgaging the house to have the building work done, just to stop the rot. My mother, as always, prevaricated and shrugged the decision onto my shoulders.

"You must do what you like, dear. The house will be yours one day. I'm sorry I can't help you but, as you know, my capital's tied up. Why don't you ask Mr Grearson for his advice? Men understand these things so much better." She died before 2008 could knock her faith by forcing her to watch all those men who 'understand these things better' scrabbling to escape the economic abyss they'd created. And we both knew her capital wasn't tied up. It had been eaten up. Apart from an annuity she used to supplement her pension, her money had been swallowed, like chunks of moist chocolate cake, by my brother, Geoffrey. She never saw a penny of it again. I will probably never know how much money he consumed, but my father's life had been well insured when he died of a heart attack aged fifty-three.

The house, my inheritance, only escaped Geoffrey's appetite for more and more cash because my mother insisted on living in it until she died. I made her a bed-sitting room on the ground floor when she became too feeble to tackle stairs. I paid for a part-time carer so that she could stay in her own home and I could work. Geoffrey paid nothing –

hardly even a visit. I became an only child. I like to think that, in willing the house to me, my mother finally said 'no' to Geoffrey from beyond the grave, knowing there could be no recriminations. He certainly looked as if he'd been slapped when he discovered that fact. And now he doesn't really communicate with me any more because his spoiled little sister has what he had always wanted.

And what do I have, I wonder? If not a poisoned chalice, certainly a bottomless one in terms of the money I have to pour into it. It's what estate agents would call 'a project' or 'a development opportunity'. There's no doubt it was once a beautiful house, I have the photos to prove it, and undoubtedly it deserves to be rejuvenated. My friends all envy me my towered piece of Edwardiana, with its huge garden, because it's classy and breathes 'old money'. They don't see the barely-holding-up fence and the broken tiles because no one gets an invitation to play in Rapunzel's tower these days. If I wanted to carry out the perfect murder, I could invite someone over and let the floorboards do the rest. Otherwise, I discourage visitors.

Logic shrieks at me, howls with the wind on a night like this, to sell up. It asks me how much longer I think I can go on funding this eccentric extravagance of a house. It might take time to sell, but I should put it on the market at once and look for something smaller that I could afford to live in. At 3.00 a.m. logic wins the contest and I make the resolution to call the estate agent's first thing in the morning. But by the morning, logic seems to be just another piece of moonshine that is out of place first thing. I know I can't go on much longer being the pathetically inadequate slave to the needs of this preposterous house. But I also know I can't sell. Only I can't explain to anyone, least of all myself, why. I often think living here has become an unbreakable habit, like smoking. My poor father considered this house his lifetime achievement. The strain of earning the money for it contributed to his heart attack. Ironically, the insurance money after his death cleared the mortgage. In a way I have taken on my father's contract with the house. It's a part of my history.

What else do I have now?

# Chapter Two

Cleaning up in the Valkyrie Suite was not how I intended to end my career but somehow my life plan turned out to be a dodgy GPS system. It led me up a blind alley and now there's no signal. I lost my real job at Grearson's, the clothing wholesalers, nearly two years ago. I say lost but, apart from the love of my life and the odd umbrella, I don't go in for losing things. My job of nearly thirty years standing simply disappeared – now you see it, now you don't. After almost one hundred years of trading, Grearson's went bust, and Prudence Baxter, Personal Assistant to the CEO, became Prudence Baxter, unemployment statistic.

I would never consider myself a victim in normal circumstances. I can't put up with the 'it's not my fault' culture. But it really wasn't my fault. From the little I've understood in reading the press reports, trying to make sense of it all, the 2008 crash was the fault of a family called Lehman who lent lots of other people's money to lots of *other* other people who couldn't pay it back. They lost all these billions because they didn't follow the normal loan shark practice of sending someone menacing round to threaten to break the borrower's legs. But how am I to work it out when even the Queen, with all the millions she's got to look after, didn't understand it? She had to ask the manager of the Bank of England for an explanation, and hopefully gave him a good ear bashing.

For a while I tried living off my savings and economising: switched off the central heating, stopped the cleaning lady and started an austerity campaign, but I knew it couldn't last. I had to look for another job, but when I began a job search it was dispiriting. The Job Centre, my first point of call, had no jobs, just a young man called Dean who sighed a lot. I tried a recruitment agency where I was patronised as a 'third age worker' but not recruited. In despair, I put an advert in the local press. That attracted replies from most of the fruitcakes in the East Midlands, but no job that was legal or worth my while. Then I had that conversation with my friend, Sheila.

On my way to the library to read the 'sits vac', I have to walk past the old lunatic asylum. For months it's been under scaffolding, but on that particular morning there was a big picture over the front of the building. I wondered if a local artist had decided to wrap it or whether someone had decided to cover up the builders' visible bum-cleavage. But a good look at the picture showed me it was just an advert for the future, which was bright and sunny and full of smiling couples, as it always is in advertising land.

"*Opening soon – The Bijou Hotel. MacAllister and Sons are realising a new boutique hotel in this tranquil location close to our business heart,*" it gushed. So I asked Sheila:

"How can it have escaped MacAllister's attention that Leicester's business heart bled to death a while ago? Hasn't he noticed the derelict factories and boarded-up shops of our delightful relic of industrial Britain?"

"But a new hotel, that might be interesting, Pru," Sheila said.

"Interesting? Why do we need another hotel? We're hardly a tourist hot-spot. True, we have got the nation's only Space Museum, and some lovely countryside."

"And Richard III," she reminded me.

"Still, I think a new hotel is a doomed venture."

"But don't you see, Pru? A new hotel needs new staff." For once I was grateful to her for stating the obvious. "This one could have your name on it, Pru."

"That's an idea," I said. "With my experience I'd make a first-class manager or, at the very least, a receptionist." She didn't comment but searched on her tablet for the site. Smart People were handling the recruitment and were holding open interviews at the Hilton Hotel, the following week.

Open interviews, as I discovered, mean anyone can just walk in off the street and ask for a job, and large numbers of us had. All human life was there. I spotted one middle-aged man but the rest all looked like they were on an outing from the local infant school. The chit who interviewed me wasn't much older.

"We're looking to fill all the vacancies in these two days. As you can see, there's been a lot of interest, so don't be too disappointed if we're not able to offer you a position." That was the start. 'Very encouraging,' I thought.

"Which area of hotel work interests you, Mrs Baxter?"

"Miss."

"Oh, sorry yes, Miss."

"Well, I believe I would make an excellent manager."

She laughed:

"Afraid we've already appointed a manager."

"Classic case of nepotism," I muttered.

"I see most of your experience has been in clerical work." I couldn't let that one go.

"Excuse me. I did not do clerical work! I was the personal assistant to the CEO of Grearson's clothing wholesalers." She wasn't going to dismiss me as a typist. "I thought I might be rather good on reception."

"Do you have any languages?"

"I believe I'm speaking one now. It's called English." I'm not usually this sarcastic on first acquaintance, but something in her manner pushed me to it.

"I mean foreign languages."

"I studied French at school." She glanced at my CV and said:

"That was a few years ago now, wasn't it?"

"Yes," I said, "back in the days when things were still properly taught and people had respect for their elders." She had the grace to look ruffled at that.

"A receptionist also needs good interpersonal skills."

"Well, as Mr Grearson's PA, I had to deal with all sorts, I can tell you, from Chinese buyers to Peruvian packers. But I won't take nonsense from anyone." She didn't seem to value those as ideal qualifications for a receptionist. She changed tack and asked:

"Are you an early riser? Perhaps you'd like to consider being a breakfast hostess?"

I'd never heard of that job title before. It conjured visions of women in gold lamé dresses, sidling up to men's tables trying to persuade them to buy overpriced champagne cocktails, which might prove difficult at 8.30 in the morning. I didn't think that was my forte at all. When she explained that it was the waitress who served the breakfast and had to be there at 5 a.m. to set up the buffet, I thought it was even less my forte.

"You might want to consider housekeeping," she suggested after that. Helen Mirren in Gosford Park sprang to mind. I'd seen that film on an outing with Sheila and Phil. I remember Ms Mirren walking up and down corridors with a big bunch of keys, telling people what to do, making sure they were working up to scratch. That seemed more me.

"Yes," I said. I might consider housekeeping.

Then she sent me off to do an aptitude test, things like: *ice is to water, as rock is to...* and making pictures from a lot of blurred lines. I found the whole thing a bit of a blur, especially as she wouldn't give me time to finish it.

"Nice meeting you, Mrs – sorry, Miss Baxter." She gave me the ends of her fingers to shake.

"We'll be in touch."

And to my surprise, they were. They appointed me to housekeeping and invited me to a staff meeting to sign a contract, just before the opening. It was only then that I discovered I'd been completely taken in. No sober black dress and chatelaine, instead, a shriek-pink sweatshirt with *'Bijou'* written across the right chest and *'A jewel of a hotel'* on the back. The ensemble was completed by a pair of matching jogging bottoms. The sweatshirt alarmed me. I didn't remember Helen Mirren sweating, even when she did the murder. And then there was the colour. I said to another woman I saw holding up the same set:

"This is not how I imagined housekeeping. I think there's been some mistake."

"I take it home, wear it for me jim-jams," she said, and cackled. "Is too good for cleanin' bedrooms dis." And that's how I discovered that Smart People were actually Despicably Cunning People, and had lured me in under false pretences to end my working days as a chambermaid.

# Chapter Three

The Valkyrie Suite is my favourite part of the hotel. In the month I've been at the Bijou, I've got used to sneaking in here for my twenty-minute break. It's been empty since the hotel opened because it's the personal suite of the co-owner, Mr Clark, and he lives in London and travels a lot. Strictly speaking, I'm not supposed to have my break in one of the suites but there's no staff room and the manager, Mr Poliakov, didn't tell me where I could take my break, he just told me I could manage my own breaks, as long as I got the work done well. Actually what he said was:

"You work good – finish all – for me no problem the breaks so many." He's Russian and his English is very telegrammatic. He's a weedy little man with a hard stare. He reminds me of Napoleon except he's blond. I keep waiting for him to slide his hand inside his jacket, or lead us into battle. Only I wouldn't follow him. He's not my idea of a manager, has none of my old boss Mr Grearson's charm and good looks.

When someone rang the doorbell of the Valkyrie Suite, at around ten thirty this morning, I got a bit of a shock and had to move sharpish off the sofa. It might have been Mr Clark, who is spending a few days in his suite for the hotel launch party. He has a key card, but I thought perhaps he hadn't been able to get it to work, and it would have been most upsetting for him to find me 'in flagrante', shoes kicked off and feet up on the sofa. I fluffed up my hair and smoothed down my sweatshirt, just in case it was Mr Clark, but when I opened the door I found Alwin, one of the bellboys, with several boxes of glasses.

"Poliakov say me bring glass Valkyrie Suite." He smiled at me. He's a handsome boy, like an actor in one of those modern vampire films: violet-blue eyes, raven-black hair and white skin. Then when he smiles you catch the glint of gold fillings in his mouth and he morphs into a James Bond villain. He's Albanian, says he's a student working part-time, though what he can be studying with his broken English is beyond me.

"So where I put glass, baby?" he asked. As an adult woman, I don't warm to being called 'baby', especially not by a juvenile with glittery teeth.

"My name, young man, is Miss Baxter," I said. "You'll get had up for sexual harassment if you go round calling people 'baby'." He clearly didn't understand, just put the box where I indicated in the kitchenette and went off muttering something fragrant in Albanian.

The glasses are for Mr Clark's private reception, up here in the Valkyrie Suite, following the hotel launch party tonight. Though I'm not on the guest list for the private reception, all we staff are invited to the launch party. I feel excited and I must confess a little bit nervous about meeting Mr Clark, because I've never met a TV personality before. *The Truth*, his programme, where he investigates all these dodgy characters, is on every Thursday. The climax of each episode is usually when he confronts the villain over his threshold, jamming the door open with his foot as he says:

"I'm Marc Clark and I've come to ask you a few questions."

He rarely gets to ask his questions because there's usually a scuffle. He's had his nose broken once. Sometimes the scumbag goes for the cameraman instead and the picture on the screen leaps and twists before going black. But a bit of rough and tumble doesn't put off Mr Clark. In fact he's become something of a national treasure for his scenting out of crooks: a local boy made good. There's no doubt in my mind that if he'd conducted the interviews personally, instead of leaving them to Smart People, he would have sniffed out my potential. I could have been manager now and shunted Poliakov over to shining shoes, a role far more suited to his stature.

The co-owner, Gavin Strutt, is also a local lad, but although he's apparently worth millions, he's not so well known as Mr Clark. I'd never heard of him, anyway. Dave, our maintenance man, was surprised when I admitted that. He told me that Gavin Strutt's scrapyard, which used to spread over the forecourt of the old Great Eastern railway station, was once famous throughout the East Midlands as a place for cheap car parts. When I told him that tinkering with old cars had never been one of my hobbies, he was even more surprised. The station was knocked down years ago and Mr Strutt has certainly moved on. Now he's a whizz-around-the-world-super-businessman with global interests, including a half-share in the Bijou Hotel.

I'm dithering about what to wear tonight. I can't afford anything new. I might splash out instead and get my hair done to give me a bit of confidence because of course, as usual, I'll be going alone. Sometimes it depresses me how completely I've failed to achieve the two main goals of my life: to get married and travel round the world. Here I am, still single at fifty-five, working in my home town, with not even the prospect of a trip to Nottingham on the cards. I do sometimes still indulge in the fantasy of acquiring a husband – not for the sex – I feel a headache coming on at the thought of it. I'd say my motives are economic and social. If I had a husband I could kiss my cleaning trolley goodbye and let said husband keep me in idleness. I could dance with him at the Drama Group annual dinner, and send him out to wrestle the bin onto the pavement on Wednesdays. He could even rehang the coat rack that fell off the wall a month ago. In fact, I could be just like all the other women of my age instead of a leftover from Gavin Strutt's yard. My ideal husband would be a collapsible man, easily stowed in the cupboard when not in use, and preferably one not too hirsute. I've had a real phobia about hairy legs ever since I had a boyfriend with sideburns. The model of husband I'm after hasn't appeared on the market yet.

Mr Clark is a very tidy man, unlike the majority of the hotel guests. The only signs of his presence in the suite are the toiletries in the bathroom and the waste bin full of shopping bags. In fact, the evidence suggests he spent all day yesterday in a one-man attempt to overcome the high street crisis. It's the bags that puzzle me. As I was sorting them for recycling – we're very green here – I noticed one of them was from Madame Claude's. I've only been in that shop once. I thought it was one of those sex party shops – like Tupperware, only rubber instead of plastic. That sort of place has stopped lurking in the back streets and strutted into the shopping centres in the last few years. Although it's apparently a legitimate ladies' undies shop, it's not my thing at all. I've always bought my underwear in M&S. Their knickers are solidly built. Madame Claude's, on the other hand, has these scraps of pink lace and satin, and as far as I can make out, the lace intrudes into very intimate parts. Not to put too fine a point on it, having one of these lace straps chafing the crack of your bum seems to me unnecessarily masochistic; something you'd wear if you were a Catholic and doing penance.

What puzzles me though, is what Mr Clark could have bought in there because he's a bachelor. It's one of the things the profiles of him always insist on, like they're trying to make a point. He's an only child, so no sister. If he still has his mum she must be at least in her eighties, an age at which I shouldn't think she'd appreciate scanty knickers. It would be a bit racy to buy something like that for your secretary or PA, if he has one. Mr Grearson used to send me a hamper or a seasonal flower arrangement at Christmas. I wonder if Mr Clark has a girlfriend the profiles don't know about. I don't read the gossip mags, except for the covers in the newsagent's. There's never anything on them about Mr Clark except what a bulldog he is in tracking down villains and bringing them to justice.

Naturally, none of this is any of my business but a little speculation about the lives of others is only human, and it does help to pass the time. Cleaning rooms pays my bills – just – but it does nothing to stimulate the brain. It only gives me permission to rummage around in other people's bins so that I'm becoming the worst kind of nosy parker: the bored woman. I've already begun to concoct a little intrigue surrounding Mr C, which goes like this. If he does have a 'significant other' and there are no pictures of or gossip about her, that must be because she's someone who has to stay hidden to avoid a scandal. Perhaps she's the wife of another, or a bimbette less than half his age, or someone who votes for the Lib Dems. Who knows? She might even be at the launch party tonight. I'll have to employ my sleuthing skills to ferret her out and decide whether I think she's worth the risk he's taking by carrying on with her.

I'd best call time and get off the sofa before Alwin comes back with more party ware, or Poliakov comes creeping around and finding fault. I also have to get back to the Niebelungen Suite, now that it's past checkout time, and hassle the couple there. I could see they were going to be trouble: wanted every last minute of their money's worth. What they don't realise is how much time it takes to erase all trace of the previous occupants from a hotel suite. This is the essence of my job, I've come to understand, because everyone wants to believe he, or she, is entering a virgin suite – if that doesn't sound too rude. And it's not done by magic. Mary Poppins I'm not.

# Chapter Four

I have to admit I can be very naïve at times. I thought my invitation to the party was a genuine one. Luckily, I didn't turn up in a cocktail frock, but I looked smart – one of my work suits – and I certainly expected to be mingling with the guests. Mrs A, my new cleaning buddy, put me straight as soon as I arrived.

"Why you no wear your jim-jams?" That's the name she coined the first day for our hideous uniform. "Hey, Miss Pru, you t'ink you no workin'?"

"Well, yes I did think I wasn't working. It's a party. I want to be able to chat to my friends."

"You got friends comin' tonight?" She paused from her glass polishing. "If you got rich friends, why you workin' here?"

I explained to her that my friend Sheila's husband, Phil, was an old school friend of Mr Clark's. Sheila had fallen over herself to tell me that one. Apparently whenever Mr Clark is in town he and Phil meet up but Sheila's never met him before.

"Moira, another of my friends, has wangled an invitation too because Matthew, her husband, is a producer for local radio."

"Local radio? How many celebrities you know, Miss Pru?"

"Matthew's no celebrity. He just happens to get all the invitations to any event with booze." I wouldn't feel comfortable meeting them in my jim-jams. I appealed to Poliakov.

"My invitation says my presence is requested not my service. I had no idea I'd be working. Wouldn't it be all right if I served drinks and such in my suit?"

"Publicity," he said. "You wear uniform."

"My clean one's at home and the dirty one's in the laundry." I thought I'd won the argument as he disappeared. But the receptionist caught me moments later and handed over an extra-large pink sweatshirt.

"From Poliakov," she said. I didn't thank her.

Sheila and Moira spotted me as I was cruising the room with *bruschetti con pesto di fave*. I was hard to miss with swathes of borrowed pink sweatshirt billowing in my wake. When I saw them my first instinct was to hide my embarrassment by skulking behind someone. The only person large enough to provide a screen was Mrs A and she was at the other end of the room, so instead I ducked into the kitchen to compose myself.

As a place to compose myself it was a bad choice. Sanjay and Giorgio, the chefs, were under pressure and berating each other. Mr Clark's favourite food is Italian and Mr Strutt's is Indian, so Smart People appointed an Italian and an Indian each as head chef in what was meant to be a fusion restaurant. It's more likely to turn into a transfusion kitchen because since we opened there's been a real alpha male battle going on. When I came in they were just hurling insults, but they have, it seems, been known to fling solid objects too and of course, in the kitchen, they both have a set of murderous chef's knives to hand. By the time I thought it prudent to make an exit with a plate of samosas – backing out to be on the safe side – Mr Clark and Mr Strutt had stepped onto the shallow dais and my friends were waiting with everyone else to hear them.

"I owe a lot to this city," Mr Clark began his speech, "because this city gave me my education and that in turn gave me the chance to go on and try to do something useful with my life." His voice is quite low, a real bass. I always thought he was exaggerating it on his TV programme – intoning like the knell of doom for all those crooks and thieves – but it seems it's natural. He's smaller than he looks on TV but still an imposing man – a rugby prop, with a full head of dark hair, just greying at the temples. If he came to ask me a few questions I'd certainly let him in.

"I often tell people I went to the same school as the Attenborough brothers – a few years after they left," he paused for the laugh. "So then everyone assumes I was privately educated, but as you all know they went to one of our city's grammar schools, Wyggeston, as did I – a kid from a council prefab." He paused again, proud and a bit belligerent, I thought, to let us all absorb that fact. "The city paid for my university education too – tuition fees and living costs for four years at Cambridge. So, starting a business here – The Bijou Hotel – in the middle of a recession, is my way of showing my faith in my home town and of putting back a little of the money the city so generously gave me all those years ago." Round of applause started by the Mayor.

"You may be wondering why I chose this particular building to renovate," he continued. "Some of you are probably thinking – he must be mad to want to put a hotel into the old nut house!" I nodded and several others chuckled. "Well, it's a beautiful 1830s building by J.A. Hansom who also designed the New Walk Museum. You'll notice we've kept the façade. It's also centrally located. But there is another more personal reason that I'd like to share with you." My ears pricked up at the word 'personal'.

"Most of you will know that this building was created first as the City Workhouse and was then made into a hospital for the insane – an asylum. Patients with all kinds of psychiatric disorders, and some with none at all, lived out their lives here." Murmurs of disquiet, disapproval circulated. Shocking what used to be done, we all agreed. "One of the inmates when this was an asylum, and one of the many who were unjustly incarcerated, was my Great Aunt Gladys. She spent forty years of her life here and died in 1968. Her mental illness? She was gay, a lesbian." People exchanged more looks at that. I could see one or two of them didn't really know where to look. Death and sexual deviancy in this very building embarrassed them.

"You all know that I am not one to stand by and let deceit and injustice win. I can't unmake history but I can turn a building that institutionalised pain and injustice, into a light, joyful place where people can relax, meet friends, or have meetings that keep the businesses of this great city thriving. In making this change, I believe I can appease the ghosts of those unhappy people who were locked away here, and finally honour their memory." A bit solemn, I thought, for a launch party. "I want you all to help give this project a great send-off with a toast, so please make sure that your glasses are charged. Whilst you are taking care of that, Gavin would, I believe, like to say a few words."

# Chapter Five

I realised Alwin was hissing at me to go over and pick up a tray of champagne, so I missed Gavin Strutt's speech as I handed round the glasses. I was still wondering about Mr Clark's judgement, in having owned up to that story about his aunt. How embarrassing to have a member of your family named Gladys.

Immediately after the toast the Sheila/Moira entourage sidled over to me.

"Whatever are you wearing, Pru?" Sheila was straight to the point. When I explained it was just a little promotion I had to do for the hotel, she said:

"Well, they might at least have found one to fit you. Who was its previous owner – a barrage balloon?"

"Gavin Strutt seems a bit of a wide boy," said Phil, her husband. He's used by now to having to cover for Sheila's 'direct approach'. "I wonder where Marc met him. I certainly don't remember him at school."

"Can't imagine he went to school much," said Matthew. Sheila laughed and said:

"You're such a snob, Matt."

"He's done very well for himself in any case," said Moira. "His company have done a super job with the conversion. Very tasteful décor." Everyone agreed.

"Strange though, this obsession with Wagner. Have you noticed? All the room names have Wagnerian connections, nothing to do with Leicester," Matthew helpfully pointed out.

"Suites," I corrected.

"I suppose you think he should have named them after famous loonies?" asked Sheila, laughing at her own joke.

"He might have chosen names of precious stones," said Matthew. "That would be logical in a hotel called Bijou."

"Watch out, Matthew's flaunting his French," warned Sheila.

"Or famous Leicester people," Moira countered. "That would have been nice too."

"Yes but there's more than one room, that's the problem," Sheila laughed again.

"And more than one famous Leicester person," Moira fought back.

"Suites," I corrected again.

"All right. Let's see how many you can come up with, and you can't have Dickie or David, cos he already mentioned them," Sheila challenged, holding up two fingers by way of a tally.

"Thomas Cook," Phil got in sharpish.

"Gary Lineker," from Matthew.

"Adrian Mole," said Moira.

"He's not real, darling," Matthew sniggered.

"But his creator, Sue Something – she's from Leicester," Moira gave back.

"Townsend," I volunteered.

"Daniel Lambert," from Phil.

"Never heard of him," from Sheila.

"England's fattest man," Moira said, and there was an uncomfortable pause as we all didn't look at Sheila.

"C.P. Snow," Matthew broke the silence, looking pleased with himself.

"Never heard of him either, but I'll let you have him, Matt, since you're our intellectual. So that's seven. It's hardly a hotel's worth. How many rooms are there, Pru?" Sheila asked.

"Suites," I corrected again. "They are suites and there are thirty including the owner's private suite."

"Twenty-three to go," Sheila taunted.

"Englebert Humperdink," Moira shouted. Matthew gave her a withering look.

"You're digging deep now," retorted Sheila.

"And there was that snooker player," Phil grabbed at a memory, "Willie Something – prematurely bald."

"Oh, I can see that one being very popular," shrieked Sheila. "Darling, I've booked the Prematurely Bald Willie Suite for our special weekend." She nearly choked on the champagne and her own wit. Several people turned to look at our group and I saw Poliakov give me one of his poisoned, ice-shard looks, and I knew I ought to get back to work, but Moira was speaking to me.

"I said he's quite a dish, your boss," I looked across at Poliakov and back at Moira. Was she joking? Unless you were a ferret fancier you couldn't possibly find Poliakov attractive. "How do you do it, Pru? First the gorgeous Grearson, now the hunk with his own TV show."

"Oh," I clicked. "Mr Clark's not really my boss. He's only here for the launch. My boss is the manager, Mr Poliakov." I pointed him out.

"Bloody hell! That's bad luck," Sheila said and knocked back the last of her champagne.

"He looks more likely to be working for the KGB or whatever they call themselves these days," Phil said.

"The FSB," Matthew informed us. "There was a big Polish and Ukrainian migration to the city just after the war, but I didn't think we had many Russians."

"He's moved here for the job," I said.

"Probably is KGB then. Better start behaving yourself, Sheila," said Phil. Poliakov returned our five stares without blinking.

"I must get back to work," I said, suddenly nervous under that frost-hard glare.

"About time too," Sheila agreed. "Some of us are dying of thirst." She threw this in Poliakov's direction, and pointedly held out her empty glass.

"See you at the book club, Pru," said Moira.

"Thursday at the RATS," said Phil.

"Yes, at the good old RATS," added Sheila.

"Bye, Pru," from Matthew, who had no future date to offer me.

I gathered up the folds of my pink tent and went about my business.

# Chapter Six

I would never have met Sheila if my mother hadn't brought home a RATS drama group flyer twenty years ago and nagged me to join. I had the perfect defence, I thought:

"I can't act." But she was ready for that one.

"They need help backstage." She read out the list of help they were appealing for. "At least it would be better than staying in all week. You'd meet some new people." She meant new men, but in that she was wrong. The few men in drama groups, I discovered, are either gay, hopelessly juvenile, or have wildly jealous wives. But in any case, to appease her, I found myself on the following Thursday at the Unitarian church hall face-to-face with the RATS.

The company were halfway through the rehearsal period of *The Rivals* with a much slimmer version of Sheila playing Lydia Languish. I was welcomed, perhaps too warmly, by the director, and designated prompt. It wasn't an auspicious beginning. The atmosphere was caustic. Glenda Oldenshaw, the director, would have been more at home running a dog obedience class.

No one in the cast dared answer Glenda back, so they flared at me instead. It was either:

"Goddammit, line!" as they faltered and I wasn't quick enough. Or, when I jumped in too early:

"I know the bloody line, for God's sake. I'm acting. That's a pause. Write it on the damned script. Here's a pencil." And finally there was Sheila:

"I don't say that. That speech is cut. How can I concentrate when you throw in wrong lines? Can't we get someone who can keep up?" It was my second rehearsal and those were the first words she had honoured me with. Accepting criticism is not my strong suit, even when it's well intentioned, as this certainly wasn't. Perhaps I overreacted.

"You can certainly have someone who can keep up," I got up. "Because I'm leaving. Whether my replacement will be able to put up with your arrogance and posturing any better than I can, is quite another matter." The silence that followed lasted just a few seconds, but it was almost as delicious as the look on Sheila's face. She'd received a verbal head-butt. "And might I suggest," I went on, taking advantage of the collective shock, "that you arm the next person who is foolish enough to agree to act as prompt, with an up-to-date, correctly annotated script?" I threw my copy onto the floor. I was enjoying myself, but I'd delivered my lines and knew that the only thing left was a dramatic exit. I picked up my bag and started my studied procession towards my coat and the door.

"I really didn't mean… " I heard Sheila splutter behind me.

"Please don't give a thought to apologising," I cooed. "But how foolish of me, of course you won't. After all, you are the star and I am merely the prompt." I swept out, and then remembered I'd left my scarf behind. Bugger it, they'd have to send it to me.

I didn't expect Sheila to ring and apologise, nor did I expect her invitation to lunch, but my outburst had brought me to her notice, and now she needed a chance to weigh me up. Over lunch she told me everything I had already worked out about the reign of terror at the RATS, and added that Glenda had said I was too sensitive to last, thereby recruiting me for the actors' camp.

I was bowled over by Sheila at first. I felt understood, valued, filled with an enthusiasm for life almost as great as hers. Her husband, Phil, was such a comfortable, easy-going man I thought, and we often went out as a threesome. Together, Sheila and I were a force. We started with the RATS, persuading Glenda to relax her stranglehold. The group began to flourish. I even made my acting debut under Sheila's direction, as Ruth in *Blythe Spirit.* Phil played my husband, Charles. That's almost certainly where our problems began.

I was never after Phil. I like him, and have always felt relaxed with him, but I was never out to make a conquest. It was Sheila who cast us as husband and wife and we did our best to be convincing, although our one kiss was chaste. She accepted us as 'mates' on a night out, but something in our rapport on stage gave birth to Sheila's jealousy. She was always careful to attack Phil, not me:

"Remember, in this scene, it's Elvira, your first wife, who should have more fascination for you than Ruth."

"That's what I'm playing," from Phil.

"That's not what I'm seeing," from Sheila.

When Phil and I arranged extra rehearsals, Sheila came too, to help us. Then there was the way she had, in the bar after rehearsals, of putting her hand on his shoulder and leaning into him. 'Hands off my husband you predatory Old Maid' couldn't have been clearer if she'd shouted it at me. I couldn't work it out. Phil, for all I know, may have hidden depths but still, anyone less likely to have an affair with a family friend I can't imagine, unless it's me. My mother, strangely enough, interpreted for me.

"It's a power game. In your shoes, Sheila would seduce the husband and enjoy having the power in the triangle. She's judging you, as she must, by her own standards." I wonder to this day where she got that insight.

There was an interval then of several years. Phil's company moved him to Glasgow. I stopped going to RATS when my mother fell ill, and after she died any kind of social life demanded too much energy. Then Sheila returned, rotund and with her kids off her hands, and made me her proposal.

"Pru, you need shaking up, and I'm just the woman to do it." She put a large folder on her dining room table, and began her presentation.

"Wedding planners?" I asked when she'd finished. I still thought it was some kind of joke. "But you know I've never been married."

"Doesn't matter. Weddings are big business and wedding planning has really taken off. You have the organisational skills to run the business. We'd be a perfect team. You can do the budget plans and spreadsheets and all that crap. I can take care of the creative side and do the selling. You've been running Grearson's for years. This will be a doddle for you. Less hours and more money – once we're established. Come on Pru, this is a chance you can't afford to miss."

But miss it I did and hung on to security at Grearson's. After a month, she gave up trying to persuade me, and then I met her for coffee one Saturday.

"I just wanted to let you know that I have invited Fran to

join me in Wedding Belles," a dramatic pause as she spooned a third sugar into her cappuccino, "and she's accepted. In fact she's even keener than I am. She's found the other £20,000 and we launch next month."

"I hope you'll be very successful," I said. She looked less than pleased by my response. "If you need any help with the computer stuff, I'm always here."

"We've got some young lad to do the website. I expect he can do the other things too." She put down the spoon and said, "I have to say it, Pru – I'm very disappointed in you. Since your mother died you've wallowed in depression. It's as if you're enjoying it. I can't believe you're brainless enough to throw this opportunity away. I always had you down as a Joan of Arc type, but you've turned out to be more of a timid wage slave."

"You forget," I answered, "I don't have a husband to pay the bills whilst I play at being a ground-breaking entrepreneur." She tossed back her cappuccino and said she had, 'things to see to.'

If Wedding Belles had thrived, my letting her down might have been forgotten, if not forgiven. But in fact they had two shaky years of business in which they made a few mistakes, including a very costly mix-up of dates, before the world recession came along and wiped them out. Sheila blamed Fran, and by implication me. If I had had the courage to march along with her, success, even against the recession, would have been guaranteed. Losing my job at Grearson's should have been the stroke that levelled the ground between us, allowing us to be real friends again. But for all our 'straight-talking,' Sheila has never said how she really feels and neither have I. And so we rub along, aware of the gap but afraid to try and fill it in case we both fall in.

# Chapter Seven

When I arrived at work at eight this morning, Poliakov was already here. Seeing management before nine or ten o'clock is always an ill omen. But it's no use in my experience trying to avoid bad luck. It's got the doggedness of a heat-seeking missile.

"Mrs A very sick," Poliakov informed me. "Is not possible work today. You clean dining room." Please and thank you don't exist in Russian, apparently. Mrs A is responsible for the public areas like the foyer and dining room. It didn't surprise me at all to hear she was sick. Last night at the launch party I saw Mrs A having a sneaky try of each of the cocktails before she carried them out to the guests. I don't think she realised how alcoholic they were. She winked at me to let me know not to let on, and I didn't tell. But I'm sure the silly woman wouldn't have been able to lie straight in her own bed last night with all that gin and vodka swimming inside her, let alone get herself out of bed, to the bus stop and into work this morning.

I saw no reason though why I should accept Poliakov's curt orders and do her job.

"Excuse me, Mr Poliakov, I am not responsible for the public areas. I am employed as a chambermaid. I clean chambers – derived from the French word *chambre* for bedroom, not *salle à manger* – dining room. There is no compulsion for me to go outside the terms of my contract."

The Tsar just said:

"Do now quick," and froze me with those eyes daring me to go on defying him. Mr Grearson never treated me like that. In all my years there he never once asked me to do anything distasteful. He was a gentleman. Poliakov is not. The receptionist, a girl I hadn't seen before, was listening and looked as if she were preparing to duck under the desk to escape the crossfire. I remembered Dean and the Job Centre and caved in. Fired with indignation, I cleaned the damned dining room – tuna and pimento trodden into the cream and gold Axminster – and made enough noise about it to satisfy my sense of injustice.

And even after that, I couldn't just get on with my daily schedule. Mr Clark wasn't to be disturbed before 12.00 noon and so I had to wait to clear up the chaos the private party had left in the Valkyrie Suite. If the Valkyrie themselves had ridden through on their Harley-Davidsons I wouldn't have been surprised: mucky marks on all my sparkly chrome, glasses and plates strewn everywhere and a terrace full of fag ends. Some wit had even made a Blue Peter-ish hedgehog on a plate by sticking fag ends into a left over piece of pâté. So now that I've finally tied the last bin bag, I'm having my five minutes on the sofa, and if Mr Clark walks in, or even Poliakov, I don't care.

Matthew's questions at the party set me wondering about the Wagner connection. I've never really got the hang of Wagner. I like lots of other classical music, but when I think of Wagner, which I don't do very often, I think of two improbably hefty figures in helmets, one with false plaits and the other with false beard, having a four-hour death by decibel contest. Usually they both lose. I do remember Wagner cost me a potential boyfriend. Mr Grearson introduced us. He was a sweet young man, I thought, secretary of the local choral society, invited me back to his flat to listen to his Furtwangler. All I said was that it was a shame that all the nice tunes in Wagner came in the overtures and what a waste it was to pay for a whole boxed set and then only be able to stomach the first two minutes. He wasn't very impressed. Told me I had plebeian tastes. I don't do criticism so that was the end of that. He probably had hairy legs anyway.

I Googled the Valkyrie. According to Wikipedia they are the female spirits who transport the souls of dead soldiers to heaven, or at least Odin's Valhalla: a sort of undertaker in armoured breastplate. Now that Matt has sown the question in my mind, it does seem rather an odd name to give to a hotel suite, especially Mr Clark's personal suite. I do wonder if he isn't trying to make some point by it, but I can't fathom it at all. If I ever meet him, I'll ask him. I didn't get to meet him at the launch party. Neither he nor Mr Strutt seemed to have any time for the staff last night. Even in that hideous pink costume, I and the other housekeeping staff are invisible. I didn't meet the girlfriend either. There were one or two young, glamorous types with yards of cleavage on show, who I thought might be prime suspects. But though I observed carefully, there was none of that secret 'couples' body language going on between them and Mr C.

Neither of the glamour girls was invited to the private party, and nor was I. Marlon was asked to do the waiting on them. I did try asking him the next day if he'd met Mr Clark's girlfriend. It's hard to know how much of my English Marlon understands, because he just said:

"You crazy, baby," and ran off. Maybe he thought I was propositioning him.

But then, this morning here in the Valkyrie, I found more indisputable evidence of a woman's presence. Amongst all the mess, I found some shirts, still in their dry-cleaning wrappers, in a pile on the sitting room table. Marlon, or that other lazy bellboy, Lev, must have dumped them there. Naturally I took them into the bedroom and went to put them in the wardrobe. The door of the wardrobe was locked but the key was in the lock, so I turned it and opened the double doors. Looking for a space for the shirts I saw, on the left, a couple of suits, some jeans and a jacket, and on the right, three or four dresses and a couple of skirts and blouses. On the floor of the wardrobe was the same neat division: a man's shoes on the left and three pairs of court shoes on the right. On the right-hand shelf there was a jewellery tree from which hung several necklaces.

I shut the door quickly and locked it. Then I remembered the shirts, so I opened the wardrobe again, took out the shirts and put them on the dressing table. I didn't want Mr C to know that I'd seen the women's clothes – mustn't have him think I was spying on him. I relocked the wardrobe door. It was probably an overreaction but I also took a cloth and wiped the key and the parts of the door my fingers might have touched. I couldn't help feeling a bit dirty, like a thief or a voyeur. I didn't know what to make of the evidence. This woman must be a frequent visitor, must even stay overnight, yet apart from the clothes in the wardrobe, she is invisible. The bed had been slept in by only one person. There were no female toiletries in the bathroom, no tell-tale long hairs in the basin or shower. And yet, if she never bathes or sleeps here, why does she leave clothes in the wardrobe? What's the use of having evidence if you can't interpret it? I really hate having so many questions and no answers.

*

I don't know what was mixed in those cocktails on the night of the launch party – but Mrs A has never been the same since her over-indulgence. She's normally what my mother used to call 'a cheery soul'. She cackles dementedly most of the time like a hen that's finally laid one. I always think 'cheery souls' fall into two categories: the ones who are cheerful because they missed out on a brain and so can't think about life, and the ones who laugh all the time because otherwise they'd cry all the time.

Mrs A is definitely a type two. She's had a less-than-perfect life. We've covered a fair few years of it in the housekeeping stores and the staff locker room. She didn't finish school because she fell pregnant at sixteen and went on to have five children altogether. Her husband ran off ten years ago with her eldest daughter's best friend. Then, on Boxing Day last year, he reappeared, thrown out by his inamorata because he had developed Parkinson's disease.

"And you took him back?"

"What I'm gonna do, Miss Pru? I marry him in the sight of the Lord. I take him for better or worse." A moment's reflection then with her natural comic timing, "I had the worse. One day maybe the Lord gonna send me the better." That was followed by a yelp of laughter, in case I might be tempted to feel sorry for her. She's genuinely religious, Mrs A. I suppose that's another crutch to lean on when life kicks your feet from under you. Not one I fancy.

Usually she's at work bright and early and heading off down the corridor by the time I arrive. The poor woman has a second job, three days a week cleaning for a lady in Glenfield, so she can't afford to hang about. But this morning she was waiting for me outside the storeroom.

"Forgotten your key, Mrs A?" She didn't offer me a smile, just a question.

"Miss Pru, they lock up the insane people in here, that right?"

"Not in our storeroom, Mrs A. The only insane people who go in there are us, working for these wages." Not even a raised corner of the mouth.

"Mr Clark tell everybody he know an old lady who die here. I heard him say that at the party," she went on.

"Mrs A, this building was a workhouse and then an asylum. I suppose a lot of people died here, poor souls." I seemed to have confirmed something for her.

"Miss Pru, you believe in ghosts – souls of people not at rest?"

"Can't we have this discussion about the supernatural inside the storeroom, Mrs A? Isn't this one of your days with Mrs Edgecombe? You'll get behind." She was blocking the entrance to the store – very effectively with all her bulk.

"Is haunted, Miss Pru." I laughed but she looked anguished. "I hear them in there. I hear them two times now. I'm shit-scared but when I go inside – nobody is there." I didn't know what to say to that. "We leave them be, that's the best," she told me. "You and me let's go and ask for another room where we leave our cleaning stuff." She seemed to be quite serious. She had a little sheen of perspiration on her face. But I couldn't let her go to Poliakov. If he understood what she was saying he'd think she was drunk or crazy and sack her. I tried to laugh her out of it.

"But who would haunt the housekeeping room, Mrs A?" I paused for my pretended light bulb moment. "But of course. It's the ghost of the fanatical cleaner who slipped on her own bar of soap, landed head first in her mop bucket and drowned. Now every morning she returns to slop that final foot of floorboards she never finished." I laughed stupidly at my efforts. Matthew would have been proud of the alliteration. But Mrs A, although she had moved from the door, was unmoved and unamused. She watched me gravely as I took out my key card and unlocked the door of the storeroom. I was a touch nervous after all that, but inside were our three cleaning trolleys, the large skip for the soiled linen, stacks of clean linen on shelves, together with boxes of replacement toiletries, loo roll, vacuum cleaner bags, in fact all the usual stuff and all exactly where we had left it, as far as I could judge. Mrs A still refused to cross the threshold and I had to wheel out her trolley and wait whilst she checked if she needed replacement items. Then she set off down the corridor without a greeting or a backward glance.

I heard her vacuum cleaner start up as I crossed to the lift with my trolley, and saw her mournfully start on the reception floor. I thought about her when I was in the lift. She hadn't liked my laughing at her, but what else could I have done? We'd have it out another day. Give her time to get over the alcoholic poisoning. Every day I have to pull the damned trolley out of the lift and every day I curse the way one of the wheels locks and has to be jumped over the gap between the lift and the landing, at great risk to my lumbar vertebrae. This morning a piece of paper 'jumped' off the trolley as I jerked it. 'That's odd,' I thought. We're devoted recyclers at Bijou, so any paper I collect from my suites I deposit in the paper recycling bin in the service area, before I put the trolley to bed. This must have been a piece I'd overlooked, which was not like me.

I picked up the offending snippet to put it into my 'paper' sack. It was a piece of card the size and shape of an old-fashioned train ticket. It was dark red, very striking, like dried blood. There was black writing on it – weird script that I couldn't read. Across the top edge someone had handwritten a number, maybe a mobile phone number. Perhaps Mrs A's ghost was trying to communicate with us and had slipped it onto my trolley in the storeroom. The phone number made me curious enough about it not to put it into the recycling sack, but pop it instead into my bum bag.

# Chapter Eight

I learned at a comparatively early age that life doesn't always have the courtesy to follow the careful blueprint we have laid out. My father succumbed to undiagnosed heart disease when I was a few weeks short of my twenty-first birthday. In my plan, he lived into wise old age. In the video of my life I'd projected at twenty, he was there walking me down the aisle, taking his grandson to fly a kite in Victoria Park, retiring with my mother to a bungalow on the east coast leaving me mistress of The Tower. In the first numbing shock after that telephone call, it was the unfairness, the being cheated out of my schemes for the future, that were the focus of my grief and resentment. Only later did I sense the value of the real treasure I had been robbed of, for I had lost the only man who would ever love me unconditionally: my truest friend.

My actual best friend, for I had such relationships then, was Helena, a girl I'd known since the first year of grammar school. She holds a special place in my recital of my life, as the first person to dump me. She was at university in Durham when my father died. She used to invite me for weekends for some diversion therapy. I was pleased when she got a job in Nottingham, for it meant we would see more of each other and could go back to the closeness of our schooldays – well almost. For about a year we spent part of nearly every weekend together. I helped her decorate her flat. We went on holiday in the summer to Italy, in search of two latter-day Gregory Pecks with Vespas.

Then suddenly, she was too busy to take time off at weekends. Her calls became less frequent, and when I called her she was rarely prepared to 'dig in' for a long chat, as she always had. I knew she was ambitious, and she told me herself that she was putting in long hours at work, and that seemed sufficient explanation for the change in her. But I felt lonely and a bit resentful and touched with a childish foreboding. When I suggested we do something special to celebrate her twenty-fifth birthday, she was lukewarm.

"It's difficult because it's on a Wednesday," she said on one occasion.

"My parents have been talking about arranging a meal out," she said another time.

"I might organise something at my flat. I'll be sure to let you know," were her last words on the topic. When there was still no firm plan a week before, I decided I'd surprise her by taking over a present and a birthday cake, and treating her to dinner. I left work early in order to arrive around seven o'clock. She opened the door to me. She certainly looked surprised. I could see that she was getting ready to go out somewhere glamorous.

"Pru. What are you doing here? I never expected to see you. Come in. I have to go out in half an hour, but come in and have a glass of wine."

"Your mum and dad decided to come over, then?"

"What? No, I'm seeing some friends. There's some red open, I haven't got any white that's chilled." She gave me a glass of pretty awful red to drink her health, but I drank alone. She carried on doing her hair. The wine went down in nervous gulps because I felt so uncomfortable. She was glancing anxiously at the clock every few minutes, and skirted round my questions.

After a quarter of an hour, I got up to go. I no longer wanted to be there since she had no time for me. My present and card lay unopened on the kitchen table next to the uncut birthday cake in its box.

"I hope you enjoy your evening – whatever you're doing," I said. But I couldn't stop there.

"I don't want to start a row on your birthday, but I don't understand why you're being so frosty with me. What have I done?"

"I can't talk about it now, Pru. You've just chosen a bad time. You know I don't like surprises."

"I only came because I didn't want you to be alone on your birthday. I imagined you'd rather spend it with your best friend." A car drew onto the forecourt of the flats and caught the attention of both of us. It was an expensive car, a black Saab, and the forty-something man who got out of it and rang Helena's bell didn't look like he had problems affording to run it.

"Pru, this is Andrew. I'm so glad you've finally got the chance to meet him." He glanced briefly at me as if I were a problem he had to solve as quickly as possible, and shook my hand.

"Nice to meet you, Pru, is it? Unusual name." And then to Helena "Darling we really must get a move on. The table's booked for 7.30."

"Don't worry about me," I said. "I'm just leaving. I've already stayed too long – about twelve years too long, in fact. Enjoy your evening."

In my video, Helena and I had had no secrets. We had told each other at once about new boyfriends and asked for approval when we had found 'the one'. We'd been each other's bridesmaids and then competed over baby's first smile, first tooth, first words. In real life, I was left standing on the pavement, in the Nottingham dusk, as the black Saab disappeared around the corner.

And finally there was Conrad, the man I almost married. Well, at least we got engaged, there was a ring which I still have. I kept it at the time out of a feeling of entitlement. I preserve it now as proof that I didn't just dream up the whole episode, although even the bits that seemed dream-like at the time are a nightmare to me now. Keeping my own company isn't my choice, but it is the lesser of two evils. It's preferable to what I've seen some women do: become a willing doormat or, worse still, a psychological punchbag, because they are afraid of the silence of an empty room. And I have to concede that it would be unfair to Conrad to say that his departure ruined my life. The credit for that has to go to me; it could even be said to be my only natural talent.

When Conrad sliced through the 'happy ever after' video I'd begun to make, he simply gave my life a defining moment. Before Conrad there had been hope and zest for life and the energy to try to make things work. After Conrad there was the conviction that nothing would ever work out again, that no one could be relied upon, perhaps not even myself, that life was a chore. I stopped making videos.

My mother used to tell me not to give up hope, that I was still young with my whole life ahead of me. She never actually used the 'many more fish in the sea' line of comfort; that would have been far too trite for her. She insisted that

Conrad simply hadn't been the right one. His name alone should have warned me that there was something strange about him. But for me, Conrad's leaving confirmed that there was an aspect of life I simply couldn't get the hang of. And this last desertion left me not just single and alone as before, but less than a whole person. So for a while I did give up hope. Then I just gave up.

# Chapter Nine

"What happened, there was a zombie apocalypse or something? Doesn't either of you androids speak English?" A voice with an unmistakably American accent was ringing out in reception just as I was leaving the staff locker room in the early afternoon. The owner of the voice was a short woman with a truly impressive hip circumference. She had her back to me so I could see her targets were Poliakov and Soraya, the duty receptionist, looking like a pair of Muppets behind the desk. Whoever she was, she was right about Poliakov. He had on his normal dead look and seemed somehow to have infected the usually smiling Soraya with it.

I read in a magazine that you always know when someone is staring at your back. It's a primal instinct for self-preservation that we all have, apparently. Before I had a chance to speak, the owner of the voice swung round to face me.

"What about you? You work here? You speak English?"

"Rather better than you do, actually." It was out before I could stop myself. But she didn't seem to notice the rudeness and went on.

"Praise be, the zombies didn't get them all yet. Finally I might get some help."

"If you'd care to moderate your tone, madam, I will do

my best to assist you," I said, "but I will not be shouted at." It was like the good old days facing down Shona Loudmouth, the ringleader of the packers at Grearson's, and the most fun I'd had yet as a chambermaid. I could see I'd knocked the wind out of her a little, so before she could get her breath back I offered:

"And now, perhaps you'd like to tell me what the problem is?"

"The problem is," she started, only a few decibels lower, "that these jerks here don't-"

"I'm sorry, madam," I cut her short, "abusing my colleagues, whilst it might give you great personal satisfaction, does not elucidate the problem, or allow me to resolve it." I thought I might have pushed one button too many by taking such a high tone, but I was enjoying myself so much I couldn't think about anything else – like getting the sack for rudeness to guests. She blinked at me for a moment as if I might be some evil vision she could make disappear, then she took a deep breath and continued, still irritated but quiet:

"I just need a store, a little drugstore would be fine – any old store. Only your zombie friends over there," she looked defiant, "don't understand English. He," she pointed at Poliakov, "keeps showing me a luggage room."

"I'm sorry, madam, that you've encountered this vocabulary problem. You see here in England we call a store a shop. Whereas a store is a place where you store things." I thought I might have pressed her 'fire' button this time but she just looked puzzled and so I went on, "We don't have our own shop in the hotel. We're far too small."

"Bijou," she said, and gave an unkind snort at her own joke.

"Our bellboy would be happy to carry out your commissions, or, if you prefer, I could point out to you one or two useful shops in the city centre. I'm off duty now and on my way home."

"Okay," she suddenly lost all her anger. "You're on. Lead me to them."

In the course of our walk to the shopping centre, Natalie Grüber-Weissbaum, native of Ohio but now resident in Boston, told me a lot about herself including the fact that she might well be the woman I've been trying to find. Despite appearances being against her – she's not young or svelte – she could well be Mr Clark's girlfriend. Naturally, she didn't come out and tell me that. It is a secret. But she did use his Christian name and say that she absolutely adored him. Before we got to the 'mall' as she called it, she told me that she had known 'Marc' for a couple of years and that she was staying in the hotel, as Marc's guest. It was her first visit to Leicester and she was impressed with the multicultural atmosphere of the small town. She told me the parts of the city she'd seen on her way to the hotel reminded her of the place she'd grown up and sighed deeply.

"Are you in the hotel business?" I asked her.

"No way. I couldn't put up with people like me every day!" She laughed. "I'm in TV, kind of. That's how I met Marc. He worked with my husband on a voice-over. We're both independent TV producers, in a small way."

"Are you here on holiday?"

"It's always a holiday being around Marc, don't you agree?" But no, she said, she was working. "We're planning to cash in on the one hundredth anniversary of the Great War in Europe. History Channel has taken up an option on a documentary programme. It's an angle on the US involvement that hasn't been done before. Marc's helping with some research, and then he's going to front the show. His voice is just great for anything serious," she laughed. "He has weight and authority, like Walter Cronkite. Marc could sell a homeless man a doormat." She stopped at an American Cookie franchise and bought us both a giant macadamia and white chocolate cookie. I wasn't just being polite when I said I didn't want one, but she told me they were to die for.

"I'm sorry I lost my temper back there," she said, "but I really do think you should have people on reception who speak English. This is England, after all. Suppose there was an emergency."

"Oh but I'm not…"

"It's cool with me," she said. "I won't mention it to Marc as you've been so kind. I'm sorry, I've forgotten your name."

"Baxter, Prudence," I stuttered.

"I'll be sure to tell him how kind you've been," she said and disappeared into Debenhams, munching on her cookie. Something about those hips sailing through the automatic doors reminded me of a portrait of Queen Elizabeth I. Natalie wouldn't have needed to go to the expense of buying a farthingale.

When I was sure she'd gone I put the cookie into a bin and sat down on one of the pretend-marble, backless benches they have in the 'mall', to digest the information. Could she really be Mr Clark's idea of illicit amour? Well, there was no accounting for a man's taste. She was older than I'd expected, at least late forties, and quite loud, and not just vocally. I thought about those clothes in the wardrobe – all traffic-stopping colours and synthetic materials. I wondered how he could possibly keep her a secret. She wasn't the kind of woman who would blend in with the wallpaper. She was very confident: not the type to worry about what others thought of her, so why would she agree to keep the affair secret? But then she had said she was married. Maybe she loved them both and couldn't make up her mind: a *ménage à trois*? That was an even better story. Perhaps she had to keep it quiet because she had a lot more money than her husband but hadn't made a pre-nuptial agreement, and so if they divorced she'd be skint? I certainly wasn't disappointed. As the heroine of the little romance I was concocting, Natalie, I felt sure, could provide me with all kinds of twists and turns to the plot.

# Chapter Ten

When I got home I found Mr Hewitt waiting for me. He is a solicitor and he had that look on his face that solicitors keep for a real crisis. He's also my neighbour. The adjacent Victorian villa was converted into offices some years ago and is occupied by a clutch of solicitors and financial advisers. Hewitt, Groves and Freebody, solicitors, are upstairs, Broadman and Cooke, wealth managers are downstairs.

"Don't worry," he said, always an invitation to panic. "No one's been hurt." For a moment I thought the tower had been blown down by this morning's strong wind and it took several glances upwards to convince me that it was still standing. He led me round to the back of his building.

In the back garden of my house there once stood a copper beech tree, almost as tall as the tower, probably planted a century or more ago by the original owners of the house. I use the past tense of the verb 'stand' because when Mr Hewitt and I arrived at the back of the building, I saw that now it was lying, brought to earth by this morning's unseasonal gale, which produced gusts of up to sixty-eight miles per hour, according to the local weather centre. Most of the once formal lawns of the neighbouring villa were tarmacked over when the solicitors first moved in, to provide car-parking space for Messers Hewitt, Groves et al. and their clients. My magnificent tree was now parked there, occupying several spaces.

"When did it happen?" I asked. Mr Hewitt told me the tree gave up its unequal struggle with the wind at a quarter past one, or thereabouts.

"We were lucky to get off this lightly," said Mr Hewitt. "Twenty minutes earlier and all our cars would have been parked there." I could see the thought troubled him. Mr Hewitt has a two-year-old Jaguar. The other cars I've seen there are all expensive models – Mercedes, Audis – it didn't bear thinking about the collective cost of repairing the damage that could have been done to them by the falling giant. I've no idea what a crushed Jaguar would have cost me, so I suppose I should be grateful that the partners had toddled off to lunch or other appointments by one o'clock. Only the office staff, who take lunch at their desks and park their cars, if they have them, in the far corner of the car park, were still *in situ* when the crash came. A crimson Ka remained marooned in a corner, trapped by the prostrate beech.

"Whose car is that?" I asked.

"It belongs to Mr Cooke's secretary, but don't worry we've checked that it's unharmed and Mrs Mason will make other arrangements to get home tonight."

"I see the boundary wall has taken a direct hit," I said. "It's a pile of rubble." It's my neighbour's wall and so was actually in good condition, six feet high, recently re-pointed and will cost a fair sum to rebuild.

"There's some damage to the back porch of the building too," Mr Hewitt helpfully pointed out. On what would have been the servants' and tradesmen's entrance when the villa was first built, part of the guttering was twisted, a downpipe had a formidable dent in it and the stucco had been pulled off one corner, exposing the brickwork. It looked like some browsing Leviathan had decided the building wasn't to his taste and had released it from his jaws.

The wind this morning came in from the north-west. A gale from the usual directions of south-west or east or even north-east might still have uprooted the tree but would have sent it crashing into my garden and kept the problem domestic. It would simply have lain about being an eyesore in the garden until I could have afforded to get someone in to chop it up, cart it away and maybe even sell it for firewood. Such are the vagaries of nature that the wind that felled it, after all these years, was itself a freak and sent it crashing into trouble next door.

I discovered that the tree-cutting gangs are having a bonanza in this part of the Midlands today. I spent most of the late afternoon, when I had recovered from the initial shock, trying to find a group that would be able to clear the mess. The best I could manage was a promise for tomorrow with my own pledge to Mr Hewitt et al. that they could continue to use my driveway as a temporary car park. I was mindful of the fact that I was dealing with solicitors in offering the latter. I didn't want a bill for on-street parking of the partners' cars on top of all the other bills about to overwhelm me.

It could have been worse, as Mr Hewitt kept saying. I have to take the optimistic view. I could have been bankrupted, and homeless, forced to put the house up for auction, in order to pay for all their expensive cars or compensate for someone's injuries. For what Mr Hewitt and I both didn't know, at least until my convoluted phone call to the insurance company, is that I am not insured against falling trees. The building is insured. If a tile rips off – as I am sure several more have – and scalps a passer-by, my insurers will stand behind me. The contents are insured against fire, theft and flood. But the tall trees in my garden have never been itemised and therefore remain my liability.

In front of me were months of cleaning rooms to repair one act of nature. I wondered if I shouldn't just follow the example of my poor tree and bow to a superior force: call Geoffrey? What I most wanted to do was to rewind. I wished I had a button that would find some super-human force to pull the tree back upright, slide the slates back onto the roof, freeze-frame the picture of my life at the time when the house was sound, the sun was shining, the sky was blue, and I still believed in fairies and miracles.

*

I went to the RATS meeting last night. I thought it would distract me a bit and I also felt obliged to turn up since I'd been appointed production secretary. That just meant I had to hang around until Sheila thought of something for me to do. We were rehearsing *Charley's Aunt*. It wouldn't have been my selection but we had to keep the common denominator low to get an audience at all. No chance of doing Shakespeare or Ibsen unless we could have Ariel hanging naked from a trapeze or Nora doing some lap dancing instead of the tarantella.

Sheila is of course the director. She's very good. Always puts on a first-class show, but always demands a lot of her cast. We threatened once to have an 'I survived one of Sheila's productions' badge made as a kind of medal. In fact her bossiness does get up quite a few people's noses. We've had some spectacular blow-ups in the past, like the time we were doing *Run for your Wife* and she interrupted Roger Mason in the middle of a long speech, to tell him he still looked like a broody penguin with his feet at ninety degrees. He gave her a few rather obscene suggestions about what she could do with herself and the play before storming off. That was the dress rehearsal. But she kept her nerve. She knows when she's got them hooked.

"Don't worry, he'll be back," she said and she was right. He came in very chastened on opening night. Now they're both kissy-kissy whenever they meet. I always suspected he had a dominatrix fixation.

Phil always gets a plum role when Sheila directs and someone always makes the tired old joke about sleeping with the director, but he is one of our best actors. In this production he's Lord Fancourt Babberley, the one who has to dress up as Charley's aunt. He's too old for the role really, but the young men we attract to the group only want to do musicals. Sheila's been banging on about how she doesn't want him to be a panto dame, more of a Danny La Rue, so everyone has gone overboard. I think every charity shop in town has been emptied of lurex and sequined items to make his costume. Someone even managed to find some size nine high heels. Then last night Susi, our make-up queen, thought she'd have a practice at making him feminine. I think she overdid it: false eyelashes like humming birds and a perfect matte complexion. Unless he spoke, or tried to walk in the high heels, you were convinced there was a rather over-made-up 1950s icon in front of you.

Susi marched him into the hall where Sheila was rehearsing the others and her reaction was priceless:

"My God," she said, "he looks like a Bangkok ladyboy," and sat down and started fanning herself. Phil's an ordinary bloke, going a bit bald, so it was unnerving for all of us to see how striking he became as a woman. He has the most gorgeous pair of legs and theyr'e not at all hairy.

The trouble is that Avril Best, who is playing the real Charley's aunt, Donna Lucia, can't compete with him, and in the script she's meant to be much more beautiful. She's a lovely girl and a fine actress, very modest, but poor soul, she just can't do glamour. It doesn't help that she's built like Olive, Popeye's girlfriend – long and thin with big joints. Susi's had several goes at her make-up but the best she can do is wholesome – like Judy Garland in *The Wizard of Oz*. So Sheila asked me, as production assistant, what I thought. I told her either we make Phil a panto dame or they have to switch roles. Avril, bless her, would make a credible man and would look more like a man dressed as a woman when she has to put on female clothes, than Phil does. Phil with a bit of voice and high-heel-walk coaching would fool anyone. Sheila went home to think about it and have a good stiff drink or two, I shouldn't wonder. It must have been a real karate blow to the ego to discover that your husband looks more feminine in make-up than you do.

# Chapter Eleven

I stayed in town yesterday afternoon, partly because I didn't want to go home and face real life, but mainly because I had an appointment with Moira. She phoned me because she had discovered that morning that the R.F. Delderfield she'd chosen for us to read in the book club next month was out of print. 'What a relief,' was my thought. I hadn't fancied ploughing through one of his improbable plots. But she was dithering about what to choose instead. I do like Moira, but she is a champion ditherer. She asked me to meet her at Waterstones. I went along although I knew in advance how it would be. She asked for my advice as we wandered up and down the book stacks looking at titles. She waylaid a passing assistant and asked for his advice too. Then finally she ignored us both and went back to the book she'd had in mind all along. She chose Virginia Woolf's *Orlando*. Talk about from the ridiculous to the unreadable. I can feel a month-long headache coming on. However, she was good enough to repay my attempts at advice with tea at Mother Preston's Tea Parlour, a mock-quaint place we often go to because it's less noisy than John Lewis and they have Crabtree and Evelyn toiletries in the Ladies. Since I wasn't paying, I could forget the diet too.

We'd been in there about ten minutes, I suppose – long

enough to order – when I saw them come in: Mr Clark and Natalie. I wondered for a moment if I hadn't just made them up. I mean it was quite a surprise to see them there. Actually, if Rupert Everett had walked in with Madonna, I couldn't have been more gobsmacked. Mr Clark and Natalie in the same place as me – at the same time. Here was living proof of my suppositions. They'd obviously escaped from the hotel, and from her husband, for a secret rendezvous. I wouldn't have thought it was his kind of place at all, but he probably thought it had the 'olde worlde' atmosphere an American from Ohio would like. She began to head for our section of the cafe, but he directed her to the table in the corner, by the window that overlooks the courtyard. Neither of them saw me. Without my pink ensemble I'm another person. I always like to sit next to the pillar and face into the cafe so that I don't miss anything, and I was glad I had followed my usual habits today. Moira had her back to them so whilst she was talking I could nod and put in the right word at the right moment, and still give all my real attention to the couple in the corner.

He offered to place her chair for her. She touched him on the cheek, a brush with the palm of her hand, and said something that made him laugh, but of course I couldn't hear it. Then they sat down. He was very attentive over the menu – helping her choose, I suppose. When she'd decided and put the menu down, he put his hand in his pocket and drew out a small packet and placed it in front of her. Expressions of pleased surprise from her, smiles from him. A present. I willed her to open it but the waitress came over for their order and blocked my view. At the same time our tea arrived, Lapsang Souchong for Moira, Lady Grey for me, and a plate of their exquisite iced fancies. That caused another diversion.

As soon as I could, I looked over to see what the present was. Surely not bum-crack knickers in such a public place? 'My God, it's a ring!' I thought. I actually said the 'My God' bit out loud, shouted it at Moira, in fact, so I had to finish my sentence with:

"These cakes are delicious." She looked surprised by my sudden enthusiasm and bit into her orange fondant with new reverence. I could hardly contain myself. He'd bought her a ring and had given it to her in front of me. How amazing was that? Over in the corner, Natalie had slipped the ring onto the ring finger of her left hand and was flashing it about letting it catch the light. She spent a lot of time staring at the ring. 'Material girl,' I thought. Finally, she got out of her chair, went over to him and kissed him, on both cheeks. That's the point at which I reached for my phone, but remembered I didn't know how to take pictures. I did hand the phone over to Moira and ask her if she could show me but she was hopeless. She just succeeded in turning the phone off. Once I'd managed to switch it back on, the moment had gone.

I missed the next good moment too. She had sat down again. His hand was resting on the table and she covered it with her own. They were gazing into each other's eyes. I cursed myself for not having read the phone manual properly. How can you be a sleuth and not be able to snap a photo with your mobile? But in any case the damned waitress came back with their order at that point. I think they're a bit too efficient there, as I said to Moira, the service is a bit too attentive. Naturally, as soon as her scones with lashings of cream arrived, Natalie gave them her full attention, which is understandable. You have to be very young and green to let passion distract you from the greater pleasures in life. The hands were withdrawn. The window of opportunity had slammed shut.

I wondered why I wanted photos. I can't remember the last time I took a picture, but it certainly would have been with my old Instamatic. It seemed important that I should have some evidence of this meeting, this illicit meeting. What was I going to do with it? If they were having an affair it was nothing to do with me. There was an idea forming that made me uncomfortable. It was like the spider in the bath. Hard as I tried to ignore it, there was no disputing it was there and much as I might hate it, I would eventually have to deal with it.

# Chapter Twelve

I think Mrs A's been avoiding me. She's always already working when I arrive and only waves distractedly at me if I call out to her, so we haven't been able to have our chat to straighten things out. With no gossip to liven up my day, this job is even more the pits. So this morning I got here extra early determined to waylay Mrs A and sort things out.

There was no one in reception – a fine state of affairs – so I just picked up my work card from the file and went to the storeroom. As I was taking out my key card, it seemed to me that, like Mrs A before me, I could definitely hear voices coming from inside the room. For a second I wondered if by inventing the ghost of the fastidious cleaner I'd actually conjured her up. But I don't believe in ghosts and the noises I could hear didn't sound anything like a woman, unless the poor soul is condemned to go through all eternity with her head permanently wedged in her mop bucket. The voices I could hear were muffled and male. I couldn't tell how many and couldn't decipher any words.

I was listening intently at the door when I saw Mrs A approaching. I started a little mime act: finger on lips for silence, other hand making sweeps for 'come here'. I could see she was very reluctant to join me by the way she started immediately to back off, so I had to flap my hand like the marshal guiding a 747 onto its stand in order to convince her to come.

"You see, Miss Pru," she hissed. "You don' believe me, now you see."

"There is someone in there, Mrs A," I hissed back, "but it's not a ghost. Maybe it's thieves?" It was her turn to laugh.

"They gonna steal me trolley? Or they gonna sell me cleanin' spray for sniffin'?" She tried to hold in her laughter but it came out as a wheezy cough. The voices inside stopped. Mrs A grabbed my arm but before she could stop me I had swiped my card across the keypad and pushed the door. It wouldn't open. I told Mrs A to try with her card. She got the same result.

"Is locked inside," Mrs A concluded, and we both looked at the door. Who would go into the cleaning store cupboard and lock the door inside? It didn't make any sense. But we couldn't stand there all day waiting to find out who the intruders were.

"Oh dear," I said in my best panto voice. "We can't get in to take our trolleys. That's you and me with the day off, Mrs A. We can't work so we'll have to go home, and the hotel won't get cleaned today." After a few seconds we heard a little 'snip' of the lock being freed inside, and the door opened.

On the other side of the door was our boss, Poliakov, phone to his ear, listening intently to his caller. He glared at us in turn but registered no emotion. Dracula leaving his coffin at dusk sprang to mind. Did Poliakov shun the night instead and spend the dark hours hanging upside down from the linen shelves? He was obviously intending to walk straight past us without any explanation, so I conquered my instincts and grabbed his sleeve. I let go as soon as he stopped. It must have been my nerves that gave me that feeling of a sudden chill.

"Whatever are you doing in here, Mr Poliakov?"

He spoke quietly into his phone then turned to me, as if he'd just noticed I was real and not a hologram.

"Washing," he said. That was all the clarification anyone could possibly need as to why the hotel manager had been locked in the cleaning store at 7.00 a.m. with one or more men and his mobile phone. I looked at Mrs A to see if she understood. She's usually better at interpreting him than I am.

"Washin'?" She mimed scrubbing her face. "Or do you mean watchin'?" She gave him the gurn of a TV addict. Both seemed equally unlikely to me and equally unintelligible to him. Mrs A is short and very round. She has a low centre of gravity, which must have helped her to do such a good job of standing her ground against the ice-blast he turned on her. Only her eyes showed a flicker of anxiety.

"Men take washing," he pronounced and these were his last words on that subject. Indicating the door he said:

"Is open." We interpreted that as 'move your backsides before I fire the pair of you'. So we went into the store and left him to wander off to reception, still mumbling into his phone.

In the storeroom, everything was neat and arranged in its usual order. A large, wheeled skip for the soiled linen was sitting at the far end of the room next to the exit door that led to the service yard. The laundry company came every other day and must just have left. The door to the yard has a push-bar opening, so I pushed it open. Nothing in the yard but bins.

"They gone, Miss Pru." Mrs A was right behind me. "I see this laundry van real close one day. Lewis Hamilton that driver think he is – nearly rip off me T-shirt the speed he was goin."

We gave up the search and began to check our trolleys and restock them.

"What do you think he's up to, Mrs A?" Mrs A shrugged:

"Maybe he fancy the driver of the van?" she sniggered. "Is not my business. I keep my nose clean, I keep my job."

"It smells very fishy to me," I said. "Look, I found this card a few days ago on my trolley." I extracted the red card from my bum bag and gave it to her. "Someone put it on the trolley when it was here in the store." She looked it over without curiosity.

"Is not English," she said. "I can't read it. You call this number?"

"No," I said, "not yet. But I think I should. Shall I do it now?" She gave me back the card.

"Miss Pru," she said, looking me straight in the eye. "You the fishy one – a nice little angel fish. Our mister manager is barracuda. Be careful or he eat you up!"

# Chapter Thirteen

There was no 'do not disturb' sign outside Mr C's suite so I let myself in. I found the socket nearest to the door to plug in the hoover, before going to collect the waste bin for emptying. It wasn't in its usual place, so I looked around for it and as my glance swept the room, I saw them: Mr Clark and Natalie. They were sitting outside on the terrace, heads together over the table talking quietly, completely absorbed. Cautious, polite Pru instantly began a retreat, discreetly retracing her steps to be able to escape before they saw her. But then the new idea that was still confined to the back of my brain began to stretch in preparation for movement and stopped me. This was a perfect paparazzi moment, my chance to make up for the café fiasco and capture their illicit amour on camera. I should be Wagnerian and seize it. The Valkyrie would. My phone was in my bum bag and I'd boned up on the instruction manual, ready for moments like this. Determination goaded me on, but had to wait whilst I fished for my glasses, also somewhere in my bum bag.

During all this eternity of fumbling, I heard the loo flush and then a smallish, blurred sort of man came out of the en suite bedroom and caught me in mid-dither, trying to juggle phone and spec case and look innocent.

"Good morning," he said and deftly caught my phone as it did a backflip out of my grasp.

"Oh, thank you. I'm sorry. Housekeeping. I'll come back later. I didn't realise the suite was occupied," I said, or something like that. I was a bit flustered.

"We don't want to mess up your schedule," he said. His accent told me he was a compatriot of Natalie's. "I'll ask Marc." He went out onto the terrace. The two heads didn't immediately react to his presence. 'Blatant,' I thought. But when he spoke they turned to look into the room and Natalie yelled:

"Hi! I remember you, come out here. We're having breakfast." The last place I wanted to be was 'out here'. I'd give myself away completely.

"I'll come back later," I replied. "Sorry to have disturbed you." I continued with my preparations to leave, but the phone and glasses refused to go back into the bag. Inanimate objects have a will of their own, I've often found.

"Prudence, come and say hello." Natalie was now 'in here' so I had little choice but to comply. How should I greet my boss, my paymaster, that is? How would he take this intrusion on his privacy and worst of all, what would his reaction be when he found out that a chambermaid had given one of his guests the distinct impression that she was the manager? In a few moments I'd somehow lost the Valkyries' determined fearlessness. I was afraid I might also lose my job too. But Natalie was gushing on my behalf:

"Prudence here gave me a tour of the malls when your receptionist couldn't help. She came to my assistance and went the extra mile – literally – as a good staff member should. You should promote her. Wait a minute, what are you doing in housekeeping? I thought you were the deputy manager?"

"Prudence Baxter," I said to Mr Clark who had offered me his hand. Instead of clasping it for some reason I thrust my security pass under his nose. He was looking puzzled, as well he might. "No, a misunderstanding. Mr Poliakov's the manager. I'm so sorry, Mr Clark, I had no idea… "

"You mean that jerk with the dead eyes and only three words of English is the manager? What kind of a joint are you running here, Marc?" Natalie interrupted. "You should promote her. She's a natural leader."

"Poliakov was appointed by my business partner, Gavin," Mr Clark excused himself. "He seems efficient enough." 'Knew it was nepotism,' I thought.

"Cup of coffee, Prudence?" the telephone catcher offered. "I'm Albe, Natalie's significant other, by the way." 'So he doesn't know,' I thought.

"Croissant, brioche?" he persisted.

"No, nothing, thank you. Very kind of you but I've got to get on with my work you see."

"Slave driver, is he?" asked Natalie, indicating Marc. "Doesn't appreciate your work, but that's men all over," she laughed.

"Not at all," I started. How the hell could I get out of this? Mr Clark came to my rescue.

"Why don't we let this lady finish? I'm sure she's got a lot to do. I'm told we're fully booked today."

"We should ask her before she goes," Albe suggested.

"Oh sure, why not?" Natalie agreed. Ask me what? All sorts of questions jumped into my head like popping corn and made me nervous, but not the one she asked. "Did anyone in your family get killed in the 17-18 war?"

"They are the American dates for The First World War,"

Mr Clark supplied. "It's connected with the research I'm doing. I told them almost every British family had casualties, but they don't believe me."

"Oh yes." It was a relief to get away with such an innocent question. "Two great uncles on my mother's side and a second cousin or something, invalided out with shell shock." They seemed delighted with my answer but I was feeling less chuffed. My paparazzi moment had definitely slipped by and instead of watching them closely for couples' body language, I was answering bizarre questions about my ancestry. Worst of all, a glance at the table had shown me that what Natalie and Marc had been so intent on was not the bittersweet pain of their hopeless entanglement, but a book of photographs of soldiers in the trenches. I couldn't escape the inconvenient thought that they weren't having an affair. I tried one last subterfuge in the hope of keeping my fantasy alive.

"What a lovely ring," I complimented Natalie. There were so many diamonds on that finger she'd never need a torch to see in the dark. "Did you buy that on your shopping trip?" She smiled in a gooey sort of way:

"That's quite a story. This," she took off the ring to show me, "is the eternity ring Albe bought me for our twentieth anniversary. I lost it on the trip here. I was distraught. It's insured but that's not the point is it? But then Marc called the hotel in Stratford and the limousine company and found it. He had it couriered here and even had it cleaned. He's such a pet." 'Isn't he just,' I thought as she stroked his cheek all motherly.

"I'm glad you found it," I didn't sound very glad. "Now if you'll excuse me… "

"Yes, of course. Thanks for backing me up." Mr Clark

gave me a warm smile. He was much more human-looking than on TV. It took a bit of the sting out of losing my story – the fact that he really was a nice man. "Feel free to carry on in there. We'll stay out of your way."

"Catch you later, Prudence," Natalie agreed to let me escape this time. "Stop by when you finish."

"Sure, we're in the Parsifal Suite," Albe confirmed.

I set about the hoovering as if attempting a land speed record. I couldn't get out of there fast enough. I'd really embarrassed myself with my silly stories. The Parsifal Suite was on Fatima's round and wherever else I went today I certainly wasn't setting foot in there.

# Chapter Fourteen

Most people would like to be considered unique. I've only ever wanted to be just like everyone else. Other girls had roller skates, so I wanted some. Nearly broke my neck trying to balance on them, but at least I was part of the group. Then when other girls got boyfriends I made sure I had one too. The specimens I got landed with were frankly uninspiring – Romeo they were not – but they kept up my status. At last when other girls got married, I too wanted my white dress and my moment at the altar. That's where my life's dream began to unravel, because try as I might, it just didn't happen.

In my thirties, after Conrad, my married friends schemed to pair me off. You might think I would have appreciated their efforts, but I came to dread Saturday nights: the humiliation of those dinner parties. I used to try to make 'getting to know you' conversation with a nervously unwilling 'date' under the fascinated scrutiny of smug marrieds. I had thought then that there could be nothing worse, but I was wrong because even more terrible than that slow torture was the void when the matchmaking suddenly stopped. They all at once collectively abandoned me. For them I was the shrivelled seed lurking in a pod of beautifully rounded, succulent peas. How could it be so difficult to join their club? I was conscious that my single state was an affront to nature, which needed remedying. As a single unit I was incomplete, inconvenient, an anomaly – like a pair of tights with only one leg – no use to anyone. Hotel rooms were doubles; restaurant tables were for two. But that was to be my fate.

Their desertion probably coincided with their baby boom, when none of them could stay awake till eight, let alone eat dinner, but I took it personally and hid away for a while. I drove my mother mad with my excuses for staying in my tower. I had an idea that the 'reject' stamp would be visible whatever finery I put on or whatever false jollity I assumed, and I chose not to exhibit it. I avoided couples altogether and went out with the few single women that I knew, mostly divorcees, who whilst cautioning against marriage were desperate to give it a second go. Driving home from one of these girls' evenings through thick fog, I realised I was just going through the motions, like my windscreen wipers – pushing away methodically but making no impression on the murk surrounding me. I didn't want the momentary space cleared in my drab existence by a night out with the girls. I wanted the supportive beam of the light ahead. I wanted a man in my life.

A time before the Internet seems far-fetched and freakish even to someone of my age who remembers it well, but Internet dating wasn't a possibility. Things were more formal and more intimidating. So, at a certain point when I decided I needed to be proactive in finding a man, I wrote off for lots of brochures and eventually joined a local marriage bureau. There's another misnomer. Bureau there was, I even visited it, but marriages didn't take place there. Despite the colourful testimonials to the matchmaking genius of the proprietor in the brochures and on the wall of the bureau, my handing over of a sum of money didn't result in my marriage. I never even got close.

My money bought me introductions to professional gentlemen. The gentlemen – they were always gentlemen and I was a lady – made the contact, echoing the proprietor's sense of the ritual of courtship. I was given their details and had to indicate whether I would accept a communication from them. The details of these professional gents were written by the proprietor, and were rather like the short descriptions of dishes on the menu of an expensive restaurant: minor works of art that raised expectations the dish, or gentleman, could never live up to. My first three gentlemen were nice, but could have made boring into an Olympic sport. The next found me boring and kept sneaking a look at his watch in the brief moments he allowed me to speak. The fifth lasted six weeks and then disappeared.

Peregrine – yes really – took me several times to his favourite restaurant in the conservatory of a village pub. On date two I discovered it was his estranged wife's favourite restaurant too. She was reported to have brought her new young love there. I didn't need to be a TV soap writer to work out that he was hoping his soon-to-be-ex-wife would see him there with me, make a jealous scene, and realise that she loved him still as much as he loved her. It rather ruined the ambience as well as the food for me, to know that at any minute I might be dragged from my seat by my hair, and battered by a woman I had never met. Recognising that this was not a free man, I was about to finish with him when he suddenly dropped me – left me waiting for him in fact one wet evening outside the De Montfort Hall. I imagined that he had finally got his wish and that his wife, recognising the pricelessness of her Peregrine, had reclaimed him. But he may just have been run over. He was very careless.

Following this unsatisfactory ending, that reminded me all too forcefully of Conrad, I declined further introductions. The emotional commitment to meeting each new 'gentleman', and the subsequent crushing of all hope, was interfering with my work. I had told no one about the marriage bureau, it was so demeaning, and so I had to find other excuses for my mood swings. It wasn't until my forties, after a dispiriting experiment – a singles' New Year's Eve party – that I felt desperation strike once again and succumbed to the Lonely Hearts column. I set up a box number and had about twelve replies. Some of them were from Neanderthals who, instead of discovering fire, had stumbled upon paper and a biro, but seemed to have little idea what to do with them. Of the others, I sifted out three and agreed to meet two of them.

If I wanted to be generous, I'd say they wouldn't score highly in self-assessment, but the plain truth is they were liars. Lawrence was well below average height although he was as outgoing and affectionate as he had said – he made a pass in the first fifteen minutes. What put me off definitively was his drinking. Clearly that beer belly had been conscientiously constructed over the years and he'd grown very attached to it. Terry, in contrast, was a moderate drinker and a very interesting man who could talk on many different topics, and did. He was into jazz, modern art and had strong opinions on local politics. The two things he wasn't into were sartorial style and personal hygiene. I could overlook the first. A duffle coat and trainers could be considered very practical items of dress. But the second impressed itself upon me so strongly that I did well to survive the hour and a half we, or rather he, chatted.

So I am left with the conclusion that I must be either hypercritical or super-odd. I've argued for years for the former. I'm just not prepared to compromise. But the older I get the more I have to accept that the latter explanation might be nearer the truth.

# Chapter Fifteen

There was a piece of paper attached to my work card this morning. After Mrs A's warning I wondered if it was my dismissal note and P45. Surely Poliakov couldn't do that? There were employment laws that even he couldn't ignore. In one way, if I never had to hygienically wrap a toilet seat again, I'd be over the moon. But with the state of things in the outside world, I needed even the pittance I was paid at the hotel. If I got the sack – better not to jump to conclusions. There was a new girl at the desk. I asked her:

"Do you know what this is?"

"Letter of boss." I did wonder why we couldn't get a receptionist who could string a sentence together with verbs, nouns and articles in the correct places, and took the paper away with me to open it.

There was no P45, just a single sheet of paper with the hotel's crest – a ring with a capital B in place of a solitaire – very tasteful and understated. A quick glance didn't reveal the words 'written warning' or 'dismissal', so I read it properly.

*'We would like to take this opportunity to congratulate you all on the first-class work you've done in helping to launch the hotel so successfully. We can assure you that*

*we have received many compliments on your behalf, and the reviews so far have been glowing.*

*In any thriving enterprise, communication has to be a two-way process and so our second motive in writing to you all is to invite you to come forward with any suggestions you may have to improve our services. We would also urge you to report to management immediately any problems you encounter in going about your tasks. In this way we are sure you will all contribute to the continuing success of the hotel.*

*Owning a hotel here in Leicester is an exciting new initiative. Now that we see what an excellent team we have in place, we feel sure that we can only go from strength to strength.'*

It was of course signed Marc Clark and Gavin Strutt. Poliakov doesn't have that many words in English. It was probably an initiative straight from a management handbook – motivate your staff by buttering them up. It's much cheaper than bonuses or incentive schemes. But at this hour of the morning, it seemed like a nice gesture: a human way of treating your staff. I felt appreciated as I topped up my trolley to start the day.

The Valkyrie Suite was still a green dot on my card. I didn't think we'd see much of Mr Clark now. He'd be too busy with his other projects. He'd been a moment's distraction from the tedium and then had high-tailed it out of my life forever, which was the usual story with me and men. I went into the Valkyrie Suite all the same to do the usual flick and vac, and the moment I stepped into the sitting room I could tell someone had been in there. I've got a nose for these things now and the room didn't smell quite right. When I leave a suite it smells fresh, new, untouched by human hand. I like to think it's the magic I work, but the truth is it's probably just the antibacterial spray. That smell had subtly changed in the twenty-four hours since I'd left the Valkyrie Suite. I wondered if the girlfriend had passed through after all. 'Who's been sleeping in my bed?' I thought and went into the bedroom to see.

I was disappointed, for the bed hadn't been slept in. The pillows and cushions were all still fluffed up and round as beer bellies. The only thing I noticed was the table runner thing that I have to drape across the foot of the bed. It wasn't quite at the distance from the foot that I had left it. Someone must have maybe knocked it off and then replaced it, without aligning it as precisely as I usually did. In the bathroom, I found the V-shape at the end of the toilet roll was very inexpertly folded, and the clincher was the toilet seat paper cover. It was all askew. I would never have left it like that, especially not on the boss's toilet. I finally looked in the kitchenette – only the Valkyrie Suite has one of those. Sure enough there on the drainer was an upside-down water glass. It was dry and so was the stain left on my gleaming stainless-steel surface. Someone had been into this suite and had tried, unsuccessfully, to cover his or possibly her tracks.

It was probably that work-shy Alwin who'd snuck in on a crafty work avoidance scheme to put his feet up on the sofa and watch TV for a while – not that he'd understand much. Determined to do a thorough Miss Marple, I set about looking for other little traces of his trespass that he might have overlooked. No bum-print or sign of shoes on the sofa. I sat down on it to survey the room. Remote controls were where I'd left them after dusting, no marks on the coffee table, no hairs on the back of the sofa. He'd been careful – crafty little devil. I opened up the door onto the terrace. There was the usual pigeon poo under the railings. Mr C would have to invest in one of those kites shaped like a falcon to frighten the little buggers off – although there was always the risk that it would scare them so much they'd poo everywhere. No, I didn't think anyone had been out there.

When I turned to go back inside I spotted the strangest thing. Mr C has a nice quality honey-coloured carpet in the lounge area, all springy and new. With the light shining across it you could just make out that patches of it – rectangles – had been flattened. The carpet had had something heavy plonked on it since I had vacuumed yesterday. What was Alwin up to? Was he storing stuff in there? It had to be quite big as the shapes were long.

Mr C's note this morning had said to report problems immediately to management, so I picked up the phone, dialled reception, gave my name and asked for Mr Poliakov. There was some delay. The new girl was puzzled because there was no Miss Baxter staying in the hotel, so how could she be calling the manager from one of the suites? When the penny eventually dropped and she connected me with Ivan, I realised I was in for an even more surreal conversation. I explained that someone had been into the Valkyrie Suite.

"Is maid," he replied.

"No, Mr. Poliakov. I am maid. I clean. I clean yesterday. I go home. Someone go in suite. You know who go in suite?" I began to wonder if Red Indian smoke signals wouldn't be clearer. There was a pause:

"Is workman." He finally suggested.

“Workman? But Mr Poliakov, what workman? It’s a brand new suite.”

“Yes. Workman. No problem. You clean.”

“I clean?”

“Okay.” The line went dead.

# Chapter Sixteen

I tackled Dave, our maintenance man, as soon as I finished my shift today. As luck would have it he was just coming out of the boiler room when I was signing out. I think that boiler room is his equivalent of my Valkyrie Suite. After all there can't be much tinkering to do with a brand-new, state-of-the-art heating system, but he spends a lot of time in there.

"Fire alarm test twelve noon tomorra, Mrs B," he said on seeing me. Then he touched the side of his nose. "Only I dint tell ya." I've told him a million times that I'm a 'Miss', but unless you speak in kilowatts or square metres you're wasting your breath. His only other topic of conversation is Leicester City, and since I know even less about football than electricity, we don't converse much. But he's a very steady, solid type and one of the few staff who speaks English properly – in his own fashion.

"I hear there's been some problem in the Valkyrie Suite?" I tried to find the right tone: mere professional interest, a need to be kept informed of problems on my round.

"Oh yeah. Wossat then?"

"That's what I'm asking you. Poliakov said workmen had been into the suite to repair something."

"I've not called anybody out and there's note bin reported," he flipped the sheets attached to the clipboard he carried about most of the time. I would have liked that part of his job – walking about with a clipboard all day. I don't suppose I'd have been much use replacing bulbs in sunken lighting or unblocking sinks though.

"No. There's note for the Valkyrie. 'E's off his trolley that one. Don't know what planet 'e fell off. If 'e's a manager I'm bledy Wayne Rooney, which I'm bledy not I can tell ya."

"Well someone's been into the Valkyrie," I insisted, "left marks on the carpet. I wonder if it was Alwin? You know, the waiter-cum-bellboy, the one with the gold teeth."

"'Aven't you 'eard? Got the boot 'e 'as." Dave knew everything. "Not seen 'is face since Sat'day. There's another one now, started today, Bulgarian, or summat Eastern European. Bledy Common Market."

"The boot? What for?" I couldn't believe it. He'd been on the staff less than a month and always seemed to have been a great boot-licker of Poliakov's. Perhaps he had been caught up to no good after all.

"Search me. Must've rattled Poli's 's cage. 'E's no loss though, shifty idle bugger." He looked briefly over his shoulder making sure the coast was clear, and said quietly, "You must've noticed how many of those gels we've got through in reception. They don't last long then they're off."

"Well yes, you're right. They don't seem to be around long. I expect they're all agency staff."

"And they don't talk."

"Well they don't seem to speak that much English."

"I was never no scholar but that lot've got less English than me," Dave agreed. "Burrit's not just that. They don't want to talk to ya. 'ardly give ya the time of day. And they don't look ya in the eye. Shifty. I don't like that," he said. Then he moved closer and lowered his voice. "Din't you see the eye one of 'em had the other day? A real shiner. I asked her – 'How did you do that, me duck?' – but she wun't tell me. She looked like she was going to turn on the waterworks so I backed off."

"A receptionist with a black eye certainly doesn't set the right tone," I said. "I don't have that much to do with them, but you're right. They aren't ideal receptionists. I wonder where the agency gets them from. I mean there's no shortage of people looking for work."

Dave stiffened, drawing in a breath as he looked over my shoulder down the corridor. "Eh up, I'd berra shift meself. 'E's on the prowl." I turned to see Poliakov heading towards us. Dave extracted a pencil from behind his ear and pretended to write something on the paper on his clipboard. "Right you are Mrs B, I'll gerron to that now," he said and walked off in the opposite direction to our boss.

I had to walk past Poliakov to get to the exit, so I steeled myself and wished him a good afternoon, which he acknowledged with a grunt. I stopped in reception for a moment and then turned back as if I'd just remembered an item I'd left behind. As I turned the corner to look down the corridor, I saw Poliakov's lower left leg and foot about to follow the rest of his body into the cleaning store. What was the fascination that store held for him?

I tiptoed up to the door of the room and stood outside listening. There were no voices this time, only the sound of trolleys being moved. I've suffered all my life from an excess of curiosity. My mother always used to say my nose would lead me into trouble and she was often proved right. I wasn't prepared to hold my nose back this time either. I got out my key card, swiped it over the electronic pad and opened the door. I pretended not to see Mr P, after all, why would he be in the storeroom, but all my attention was on him. He was hanging off the skip containing the soiled linen, riding it towards the push-bar exit.

Even Sheila would have had to applaud my naturalistic acting as I gave a great start and said:

"Mr Poliakov, you gave me such a shock!" But in fact he was the one in shock. He jumped off the skip as if I'd shoved a cattle prod somewhere potentially very painful, and stood staring. I'd never seen his eyes so wide open. You could look into them and almost see the wheels and cogs turning in his brain, as he wondered how to react. I pre-empted him:

"I must be having a senior moment. I went off and left my phone in here," and I started searching my cleaning trolley for the phone that I knew perfectly well was in my bum bag. And then, wouldn't you know it, the little bugger went off. It has a single ringtone that sounds like a real phone, only people hardly ever ring me, so whenever it starts up it genuinely makes me jump out of my skin. "Can you hear a phone?" I tried to recover and look innocent, whilst continuing my search. "Is it your phone, Mr. Poliakov?" He'd got control over his thoughts and his eyes showed their normal lizard, unblinking stare. He stood for a moment watching me and my antics, then impatiently jabbed a finger towards my middle and said:

"There!" I stopped my search and let my gaze drop to the bag, where the phone was still shrilling.

"What an idiot you must think me, Mr Poliakov. It was here all the time." I tried a laugh, but it came out very theatrical. The amphibian stare held me for a moment then a change came over his face. Wheels and cogs had delivered their assessment of the situation. I was a devious cow who was not to be trusted. The stare grew into a force field that propelled me steadily back towards the door. This room had some fascination for him – a personal fetish or something clandestine he wanted no one to know about. My presence was intrusive and unwanted. He left me in no doubt that my card had been marked.

# Chapter Seventeen

My mother always used to say that trouble comes in threes. I've never noticed it being so considerate as to limit itself in any way, but when I got home there were exactly three letters waiting for me, making a random pattern on the doormat. Three letters, and not even an advert for double glazing to divert me. Two of them had the Tudor rose emblem of the City Council on them and the third was postmarked Loughborough: HQ of the tree surgeons I'd used to dispose of my unfortunate windfall. There was no point in putting it off. I would make a cup of tea and then sit down with them and open them one by one.

The first one, from the Council, informed me that they were unable to support my application for a Historic Building Grant to repair the roof of the tower. It was a blow, but not an unexpected one. My house is a landmark in the area. It's on the Local Asset Heritage Register but I never held out much hope. There's little enough money for essential services, let alone conservancy.

The second letter from the Council was obviously a knee-jerk reaction to the complaints of my neighbours about their gap-toothed wall. In an effort to keep costs down, I had offered to find someone to rebuild the wall. I had spent the weekend after the incident gathering and stacking reusable bricks and sweeping the mess into neat piles, so that they could at least use their car park. But of course I had done nothing since then about contacting a mason. This letter reminded me of my obligation, advised me that since I lived in a conservation area, the materials and style of the rebuild needed to be consistent with the original construction. It designated some helpful chap in the planning department to contact should I have any questions. I had a whole raft of questions, but not ones that I felt anyone in the planning office would be able to answer – is there a failsafe way to rob a bank, or what's the number of next Saturday's winning lottery ticket?

The third letter was Mr Brian Garstang's presentation of his bill for services already rendered. He had also helpfully enclosed an estimate from his company, A Cut Above, for the work that still needed doing to make the remaining trees safe. The sum requested for a couple of hours' work by two men would take me a month to earn at the Bijou. Mr Garstang was kind enough to remind me that, since I was living in a conservation area, I needed to check the regulations about the pruning of the trees in my garden and get the necessary permission, before he could start work. Otherwise, he or I or both of us could incur a fine.

I could hack into my 'rainy day' fund to pay the tree surgeon and hope there would be enough left in there to pay at least part of the cost of putting back the wall. But that would leave nothing at all to shore up the tower. Not for the first time, I thought about remortgaging the house. I had all the quotes and figures in a folder somewhere from the last time I'd had the idea and had gone so far as to talk to the bank. I'd been on my PA's salary then but still hadn't felt it was feasible. How would I ever make the repayments now on what the Bijou paid me? The other solution that always suggested itself at these awkward moments roused itself once more. I could contact Geoffrey. I could contact Geoffrey and say what? I could ask him for help. Certainly not, but I could ask him if he wanted to buy the house. Possibly I could do that.

I went into the living room where I kept his contact details locked away in the drawer of my mother's writing desk. I often thought there was something Freudian in my choice of hiding place for Geoffrey's 'remains'. The one photo I still had of him, a wedding picture of him and Chrissie, was also in there, together with the last letter he ever wrote to me. I didn't need to look at either of these in order to take out his phone number, but I found myself looking them over. The phrases in the letter that my mind had highlighted the first time I had read it, jumped out at me once again. '*Taking advantage of the situation*'... '*preying on the emotions of a sick woman*'... '*outrageous will*'... '*final severance between us*'... I didn't go on. I folded up the letter and put it away once more, taking care to place it over the photo and so blot out his smug wedding face. The phone number could stay where it was. I didn't need it. There had to be some other way of finding the money. Perhaps I could ask for some overtime.

*

Had a quick pow-wow with Mrs A about Poliakov's odd behavior this morning. She wasn't very supportive, I must say. I explained to her all that I'd discovered in the Bijou, which she didn't seem to think amounted to much, and then I referred her to the letter about flagging problems with management.

"I can't complain about Poliakov to Poliakov, but if Mr Clark's staying here tonight – look there's a red dot on my work card for the VS – then I can tell him."

"You sure somebody went in the room?"

"Suite, Mrs A. Yes. And no one can get in without a key card that's been activated by reception that day."

"Maybe Poli just forget who he send in. He in happy land." She mimed smoking a joint.

"Well, even if he did forget," I argued, "what's he up to in here? It's twice now we've caught him."

"Could be his mother was a washer woman so he likes to smell sweaty sheets. I don't know, Miss Pru. The Lord make us all different. He have his reasons." Mrs A was still intent on avoiding the issue and the trouble that might ensue.

"And then there's all those reception girls who come and go. Dave said there was one with a black eye. Did you see her?"

"Poor fool got herself a bad man. Is not the only one," Mrs A said.

"But what about Alwin – here one minute, teeth glittering, and gone the next. You can't fire staff just like that, except for serious misdemeanors. It never happened when I was at Grearson's, unless someone was caught stealing." Mrs A sighed:

"Miss Pru. The hotel don't belong to you or me or Dave. Is not our problem. We just do our work, they give us the money. We see nothin', hear nothin', say nothin'."

I've never got the wisdom bit about the three wise monkeys. If it really was clever to be deaf, dumb and blind, why were we given our senses? I might have asked Mrs A for the Lord's point of view on my question, since she seemed to be on such good terms with him, but she made it clear that the conversation was over as far as she was concerned. I knew I should adopt her pragmatism, but I also knew that I wouldn't. I would have to go and see Mr Clark. I didn't want to make accusations about Poliakov without being face-to-face with the boss because Mrs A was right about one thing, at least. My evidence was far from concrete; in fact it was more in the nature of fairy dust. But my gut feeling said, 'Pursue it, Pru' and I always follow my gut.

# Chapter Eighteen

I tried three times to catch Mr Clark whilst I was at work but he was always out. When I got home I found I couldn't just leave it for another day, so I decided to go back to the hotel that evening. I put on a smart skirt and top and a spritz of scent. I took my camel coat and my mother's crocodile-skin handbag, and returned incognito to the hotel. Looking smart would lend weight to my arguments. No one would take me seriously in my pink jim-jams. In reception the evening girl, Vera, was enslaved by her computer screen so I didn't have any awkward questions to face about why I'd come back to the hotel. I took the stairs to the Valkyrie Suite. At just a few minutes before seven, feeling excited and expectant, I rang the bell outside the suite. The door opened instantly, but there was no one behind it and no one in the living room. Mr Clark must have opened it from one of the consoles somewhere in the suite. His voice came from the bedroom.

"You're a little early," I heard him call from there. "I'm still not sure what to put on. Come and help me choose." Before I had time to call out, just to say that I didn't believe I was the guest he was expecting, he appeared in the bedroom doorway.

It would be hard to judge which of us got the greater shock. Chambermaid, Prudence Baxter, middle-aged employee, now disguised in smart, civilian clothes, was not the person he had anticipated. Mr Clark, in turn, although he was indeed Mr Clark, was not at all the figure I had anticipated, because he had in fact become a she. The person before me had dark auburn hair, cut in a jaw-length bob. The brown eyes, now open wide and staring at me, had their lids coloured with lilac shadow. Navy mascara tinted the impossibly long and curled eyelashes. Blusher failed to contour the squareness of the face, but the neck and shoulders shone under their shimmer of bronzing powder. He/she was dressed in one of those knee-length silk and lace slips that Tennessee Williams' heroines languish about in, looking sultry. The robust legs were encased in nylon and the feet disappeared into low-heeled, spangled mules.

"What the fuck?" the vision spluttered on seeing me, and I couldn't have agreed more.

"Do you mind if I sit down?" I managed to articulate, because I noticed I'd already subsided onto one of the sofas. Moments passed in mutual staring. I didn't know how to go on. I needed to tell him of my suspicions about the manager of the hotel. I remembered the clothes I'd seen in the wardrobe and my fantasy of his secret girlfriend. I had never once suspected, innocent idiot that I am, that he and the girlfriend were in the truest sense, one. I found I couldn't adjust to the idea. The image of the bum-crack knickers flashed before me. I wondered if he was wearing them: all that manhood straining against the lace. I suppose it was the shock, or the embarrassment and certainly the images of the intimate lingerie that my unruly mind kept flashing before my eyes, but I found myself starting to laugh, then howling with laughter. For a few moments I was helpless. I think you could have stuck pins in me and I'd have felt nothing.

Looking back on it now, I can't believe how rude I was. He must have thought I was laughing at him, at his appearance, at the idea of him pretending to be a woman. He wasn't to know that what really made me laugh was my own stupidity, my not having been able to put two and two together in a more creative way.

"I think you'd better leave," I heard him saying in that doom-laden voice and it sobered me up.

"I'm terribly sorry," I started to say, "but the door was open and..." I found I couldn't look at him. I got up to leave.

"No, wait," he called, as I was on the threshold. "I can't let you go like this." I half-turned and muttered something again about being sorry and having to go. It was hard to get words out. Then I felt my arm being grabbed and I was pulled back, with unfeminine force, into the room. The door was slammed shut.

"Sit down," he ordered. I sat like a well-trained dog and searched my bag for any kind of impromptu fan. I found a leaflet about Zimmer frames and flapped at myself with it. He sat down too on the sofa opposite. The silk slip rode up revealing square knees and well-muscled thighs.

"I'm sorry, I hope I didn't hurt you?" he said.

"No, no."

"I really am sorry but I don't remember your name," he went on.

"Baxter, Prudence, Miss, housekeeping."

"Ah yes, housekeeping. Look this isn't quite the way it seems, you know." He was smiling though it looked painful. "I'm sorry if I gave you a shock just now. The thing is, I wouldn't want you to get the wrong idea about me."

"I just came because of the letter, you know?" I twittered.

"These clothes, they're a disguise. I'm trying them out. It's for a programme I'm researching," he continued. "I need to see how convincing I can be as a woman."

"You asked us to let you know about problems in the hotel. Only it's a bit delicate, so I wanted to speak to you personally." We both continued to follow our own train.

"I wouldn't want you to think that this is something I do every evening. I don't want you to get the idea I'm doing this for pleasure." He gave a hearty laugh, which made me jump. I started to giggle a bit to keep him company. It felt like we'd reached an understanding. In fact he said:

"I feel sure you understand, Mrs umm…"

"Baxter, Miss."

"Yes, Miss Baxter."

"Yes." Then the doorbell rang. We both sprang up, but he made no move to open the door, just stood looking at it.

"There's someone at the door," I felt I had to point out. "Shall I answer it?" He gave me no reply, just sighed and looked suddenly very tired. The bell rang again – a little carillon. I was going to leave anyway, and since the only way out was through the door, I went over and opened it.

A very tall woman with long, crystal, pendant earrings and a coat with a wide fur collar, was checking her make-up in a compact mirror. She said:

"I'm not late, am I?" Then the voice faltered and left me rather confused because it was the voice of Sheila's husband, Phil. When I looked carefully I saw that under the wig and make-up the face belonged to him too.

"Hello, Phil," I managed. He didn't respond. "I'm sorry, I really have to go," I said, picking up the Zimmer frame leaflet.

Mr Clark didn't make any move to detain me. I pushed past the still silent Phil and made for the stairs.

It was only as I was crossing the road outside the hotel, worrying about Phil and Sheila, that a thought hit me, and nearly buckled my knees. This was the sinister spider spinning a web across my brain that I hadn't been able to face or to dismiss. Mr Clark was a celebrity and that made him vulnerable, exploitable. And he had given me a story: a real tabloid headline story. This was a goldmine. Solid, upright, macho Marc Clark, defender of the honest citizen, becomes in his spare time, not Superman, but a screen siren, and squeezes into bum-crack knickers and satin slips for a tête à tête with the delicious Phil. But of course I wouldn't mention Phil. The tabloids would be paving my driveway with twenty-pound notes to get their hands on this one. That many notes would pay for the wall and the tree-felling and the repairs to the tower – I might even get an exotic trip out of it. All I had to do was go home and ring the press.

# Chapter Nineteen

Most people I know would laugh themselves silly at the thought of me lacking confidence or being low in self-esteem, but that only shows how little they know me. Or rather it shows how little of myself I've chosen to reveal to them. For the image I project, I have to admit, is of a strong, independent woman. They don't see that my attack, my criticisms, are a frontline defence, my armour against vulnerability. Perhaps I was born with this personality. I certainly don't remember a time when I wasn't like this, except once. I prefer to lay the blame for my insecurity on the two men in my life who taught me how much pain can be inflicted on you if you ever, for one moment, lay down your shield.

In one of my earliest memories I'm in a green space surrounded by giants. The giants keep pressing down their faces towards me and perplexing me with their questions. I'm not crying. I'm too afraid and I know that I have to concentrate because the questions are important. Gradually the face of one of the giants begins to look familiar. It smiles and I'm given chocolate buttons to eat. They are round like the faces and mouths and eyes surrounding me. I pop one into my mouth. As it melts I am back with my mother and she is hugging me.

When I asked her, years later, if that was a real memory, she laughed and said:

"That must have been the time Geoffrey left you in the park. He met some of his friends and went off to play, and forgot you. A neighbour brought you home."

"How old was I?"

"About three or four, I suppose."

"So he would have been eight or nine?"

"Yes."

"And he just dumped me."

"Of course not. He got a bit distracted as children of that age do."

I still stick by my interpretation of the event. He left me like a piece of litter he had deliberately dropped, hoping someone else would dispose of it. Siblings fight: it is part of the natural order of things, prepares us for the bigger knocks of life. But with Geoffrey it was hard to fight back. He was a selfish, cunning bully, who never lost an opportunity to let me know that I was smaller, weaker and much less intelligent than he was. In our childhood, even into early adulthood, he left me in no doubt that, in his view, I didn't merit a place in his family.

Geoffrey got good grades and went away to London to study. I had lovely, long breathing spaces during his term times. I was fourteen going on fifteen. I'd grown suddenly. Every bit of me seemed to have a sharp point – not just my tongue. My vaguely red hair wouldn't cascade in waves over my shoulders. It couldn't cut into a neat bob, so it was sliced very short. I had the sense of looking like a long stick of rhubarb that rapacious caterpillars had comprehensively nibbled at one end. I didn't enjoy the breathing space of

Geoffrey's university years as much as I had imagined I would. My mirror tormented me instead.

Eventually, I also got good grades, but only in girly subjects like English and History. I didn't go to university. Geoffrey had by this time moved away permanently and so I had no incentive to leave home. The truth was, I was too scared. I stayed at home and went to secretarial college, and when my father died the following year, I had no choice but to stay put, with my mother, and work through my grief. I told myself I felt comfortable in my home town: I didn't. I fooled myself that some wonderful man would materialise to save me from the tedium: he didn't.

PA to the managing director of Grearson's was only my second job and I counted myself one of the blessed to have got it. I felt as if I were crossing the threshold into a bright, new future. And then Conrad entered my life and not only switched out the light, but stole my torch too, the bastard.

At the time of Conrad, I was having my brief moment of being in fashion. With my big hair, my cropped, fitted tops and long skirts that covered my scrawny legs, I was at least presentable. But I must have been the dullest young woman he'd ever encountered. I took care that he never saw the abrasive Pru. I was so pathetically grateful for his interest in me, so convinced that he was 'the one' that I didn't dare risk showing him real feelings. Instead I studied his taste in everything to the finest detail and then mirrored that taste to the finest detail. It never occurred to me that I was defrauding him. After all, he got engaged to a woman he didn't know.

On the other hand, I was deluding myself, and I had no idea of that either. I was happy. He had proposed, we'd set a date for the wedding, everything in the fairy-tale was on script. I was about to reach that moment when I could relax my endless vigil as a single woman seeking a mate, and pass into the calm, security of belonging to someone. Then, just as I was about to sink my buttocks into the squashy cushions of that comfortable armchair of marriage, Conrad pulled the whole thing from under me.

A weekend away in the Cotswolds: a great chance to talk through the wedding plans.

"I may have to take a few phone calls. The project at Cirencester is behind schedule. The builders will be there all weekend." He was a civil engineer working for the Electricity Board. He often had to 'check in' at weekends or rush off to an emergency. I was used to it and never questioned it. I accepted everything. On the Saturday we were out all day and didn't get much done in the way of planning.

"We've still got time tomorrow," he said. But we hadn't. After breakfast he said, "I have to go over to the project. I'm sorry but it's urgent."

"It's all right. I'll come with you. It's a lovely day. I'm sure I can find something to do whilst you are working."

"No," there was to be no discussion. He was immoveable. "I've called you a taxi. You can get a train back from Oxford. I'll probably have to stay at the project overnight. Can you be ready in ten minutes?"

As my taxi was turning out of the hotel car park, it was almost hit by a white Ford being driven by a woman with bright red hair.

"Bloody women drivers!" grumbled the driver. "Sorry, no offence. Going somewhere nice, are you?"

The perfunctory kiss as Conrad had put me into the taxi was in fact our big goodbye scene. I just didn't know it and so

I missed it. For a week I heard nothing from him. He didn't phone and I couldn't get any reply to my calls. I dialled all the numbers I knew for him, including some of his friends, and finally a note arrived. I tore it up, sealed it in an envelope and posted it back to him. Now I wish I hadn't done that. I wish I still had the proof of what a bastard he was. It said:

> *'Please don't make this harder than it already is. I can't see you again. Please don't phone me or my friends. I'm in love with someone else. Try and be happy.'*

Or something like that. That was the gist. I may have missed some of the embellishments, but I'm quite sure the word 'sorry' wasn't anywhere on the page. I had no idea what I'd done to provoke such cruelty, but I knew what I had to do – strap on my armour and clank back into my tower.

For most of my life I had believed that the redhead in the white Ford was the 'someone else' and had pictured their life together. But again I was wrong. After my mother's death, I went one Christmas to a friend's party and met a man who had worked for the Central Electricity Generating Board. He was entertaining us with stories of his ex-colleagues and finally came to the one about the man who collected redheads. It seems this amusing Don Juan had had a girl in every town in which he had worked, and he'd moved around a lot. He referred to them all as 'projects' and managed somehow to keep them all in ignorance of each other. Got away with it for quite some time, but then:

"He'd just got rid of one of the girls, waved her off in her car, and another one screamed into the driveway in her sports car. She'd found out he was seeing someone else and started smashing into his car. He had to get the police to call her off. Did over £5,000 worth of damage." 'And not just to his car,' I thought.

"What happened to him?" I couldn't help myself as the laughter around me died away.

"That's the real joke. Married a brunette – right dragon of a woman by all accounts. He was running a bar in Majorca the last I heard."

# Chapter Twenty

'I beg you, Pru, don't say anything to Sheila before we talk. When can we meet?' was the first text I got from Phil just after I got in last night. It answered one of my questions: Sheila doesn't know. How does he get out of the house dressed like that? Even if he waits until Sheila has already gone out, the neighbours might see him and comment. And where does he keep all those clothes and the wig and make-up, I wondered – in his office? Anyway, Phil's problem was secondary to my concerns. I could sort out my loyalties there later.

What I had to do as soon as I got in was phone some newspapers and get them interested in the story: Marc Clark in women's knickers. It was a pity I didn't have any photos. Pictures convince much more than words. I hadn't been quick-witted enough. Would the newspapers just take my word for it that he was a transvestite? Was that even the right word? I obviously couldn't call upon Phil to back me up without asking him to drop himself in it too. And if Mr C had any sense, he would dump the clothes and make-up well away from the Valkyrie Suite and deny everything.

"First things first, Pru," I said to myself and went online to find some numbers. I was unusually slow. My fingers jumped about and couldn't seem to hit the right letters. But eventually I had a list of numbers. I thought I'd start with the *Mail.* It seemed like their kind of story. I jabbed at the numbers on the phone pad and got a silence. I must have misdialled. I tried again and this time got one of those infernal menus. I put the phone down. I couldn't cope with decisions, I just needed to tell someone the story – no names of course – and ask how much I'd get for it. A simple matter of business. I needed money and had something to sell. There was sure to be a buyer.

"Come on, Pru, don't dither," I chivvied myself. "Would Wagner's Siegfried let a menu put him off? Would he give a damn about how much he intruded and messed up the lives of others? No he would not. He'd trample everything in his path to reach his objective." I picked up the phone again and got as far as hearing a real human voice before I put it down again. It was no good. I wasn't Siegfried. I couldn't trample. All the bluster, the outer hardness, my attempt to be the 'Shona Loudmouth' of the Bijou Hotel counted for nothing, for I always came home to Prudence Baxter.

I switched off both my house phone and my mobile. Phil's messages were clogging up the inbox. He'd have to stop soon. He couldn't sit up all night texting; Sheila would think he had a mistress. He'd have to go to bed as normal. I went to bed, but it was a waste of time; I had no chance of sleeping. Siegfried wouldn't lie down. The tower, that great stone phallus lurking in the dark, demanded action and strength on my part. I couldn't just let it crumple into a heap. It was insistent. A little firmness on my part was what was needed: rigid determination. Looked at from the perspective of those badly needed building funds, what was Marc Clark to me? He was a fool, a man prepared to risk the career and solid reputation he'd built for himself, for what: an hour-or-so's titillation? Wasn't that men all over for you? Why should I worry about one particular specimen of the sex who couldn't even remember my name – a man who had lied to me, even manhandled me in order to keep me quiet? He didn't deserve the consideration I was currently giving him. At 3.22 a.m., I got up, determined to switch the phone back on and make that call, but when I got downstairs I skirted the telephone and made a cup of tea instead.

Something stronger even than Siegfried held me back, stood, hand raised, telling Siegfried to go and take a cold shower. I reflected that it would have been easier for me if Mr Clark had been having a sordid affair. Then I could have concentrated my anger and contempt on him and the floozy: the little gold-digger with her claws into a man more than twice her age, the bored mid-lifer cheating on her adoring husband. When it was just Mr Clark living out his fantasy by dressing up as a woman, the moral anger refused to be provoked. I couldn't let go of the image of him in the Valkyrie Suite: a middle-aged man, vulnerable in his lilac eyeshadow and satin slip, looking like a kicked dog. He was so depleted, so insubstantial at that moment with all the knowledge of the weakness of his position, that I could have brushed him with my makeshift fan and he'd have disintegrated, leaving only the slip, the wig and the mules in a pile on the floor. No one had the right to diminish another like that. I had done it to myself over the years and now I'd done it to him by laughing so helplessly. I had given him the conviction that I couldn't be trusted to keep his secret, but would hold him up to derision by broadcasting the story as soon as I was out of the room. And wasn't his conviction right? Hadn't I skipped along the pavement outside the Bijou, clutching at imaginary sacks of gold, and sped home to call the tabloids?

When my alarm went off upstairs at 6.00 a.m. I was still nursing the dregs of my cold tea and facing a day that already looked to me like the brown murk at the bottom of my mug.

# Chapter Twenty-one

I was late into work. My attempt to creep unseen past reception was thwarted. The girl at the desk handed me my work card: no attempt at a smile. She's not paid to exercise her face muscles for the staff. She grunted at me instead to point out the envelope attached to the card.

"You Baxter – for you." An envelope with my name in big, scrawling handwriting. I didn't need to have seen the signature on the photocopied letter to staff, to know that it was from Mr Clark. I took refuge in the cleaning store to read his note. Since I was late, Mrs A was already working, the ghost had come and gone and I'd missed Poliakov's tryst with the dirty linen and/or the van driver, and so there was no one to interrupt me as I read:

*Dear Mrs Baxter,*

*I believe you had matters to raise with me that we were unable to discuss at our hurried meeting yesterday evening. If convenient to you, I suggest that we meet at four o' clock this afternoon to discuss your concerns and other important matters.*

*Are you familiar with Ma Preston's Tea Rooms off Highcross? I suggest this in preference to the hotel as a quiet location where we will not be disturbed.*

*In the event of your having a previous commitment, I would ask you to phone me at the number below to make another appointment. I am most anxious to speak to you before I leave for the States on Sunday.*

Someone else hadn't got much sleep last night either. It was a very careful note that gave nothing away and even made it seem that I was the one with problems to resolve. He was clever – the city council hadn't wasted their money on those four years at Cambridge after all. Just not clever enough to keep his secret life a secret. I would meet him at four and I made a little pledge to myself. If he tried to fool me and came up with another silly cover story for his cross-dressing, then he himself would have given me the green light to talk to the *Mail*.

I waited until I took my break, when Phil would be safely at work, in order to reply to his thirty-one texts and missed calls. I had sat down on the sofa in the Tannhaüser Suite and was reflecting that I couldn't cope with lack of sleep. Even flicking a duster this morning felt like building a pyramid single-handed.

Phil answered instantly and was obviously within earshot of work colleagues.

"Miss Baxter, how kind of you to call back. Have you spoken to my … to er… to the director yet?"

"Morning Phil – I presume you are Phil this morning? Of course I haven't told Sheila. You must know that's your job, not mine."

"Yes, well that might be difficult."

"I just wanted to let you know that I'm not going to blab or gossip."

"Thank you! It's certainly good to hear that."

"But that doesn't mean you're off the hook. I don't think it's fair to Sheila to keep her in the dark like this. And you put me in a very awkward position. How can I act normally when I see her, knowing that I know something about you that she doesn't?"

"Yes, I do understand your position. I suggest that we meet at the earliest opportunity to have some clarification on that point."

"I'm meeting Mr Clark this afternoon at four."

"A very sound idea but I'm afraid I can't make it then. I was going to suggest tomorrow evening at six in the private bar of the Wheatsheaf. I have another appointment close by at seven."

"It's RATS at seven. Won't Sheila think it strange if you don't go home first?"

"Not at all. I often work late on Thursdays."

"Two dates in two days," I said. "I've never been so popular. All right, I'll see you then."

"Thank you for your understanding. Until tomorrow. Goodbye."

*

The Tannhaüser is the smallest of the suites I do and has a quirky shape. The bedroom is almost triangular. It's a bugger to get the vacuum cleaner into those angles. I was very tempted this morning to cheat and just mark it as 'serviced' on my work card. It had been empty last night and didn't have another booking until the weekend. As I got up off the sofa to leave, my phone tumbled onto the floor because I hadn't zipped up my bum bag properly. Luckily the carpet in there has a thick pile so there was no harm done. Stooping down to pick up the phone, I noticed something on the carpet: the same strange marks that I'd seen in the Valkyrie Suite. They were harder to see here because the carpet had a fleck in it, but they were definitely there: at least two long, rectangular indentations.

I went into the bedroom – everything was as normal there – and finally into the bathroom. There I found a similar amateurish folding of the toilet paper and no toilet seat cover at all. It had disappeared. The bath and sink were both dry but the shiny surface I always leave on the porcelain of the sink was covered in water stains. One of the towels was missing. I automatically picked up the phone, then put it down again. There was no point in calling Mr P. He'd been evasive the last time. Either he was actively colluding in what was going on, or he knew something but didn't want to admit it. I would check with Dave and keep this latest evidence for Mr C himself. And that settled it: I wouldn't clean the suite but leave the crime scene exactly as it was.

On the point of leaving I gave the room one last sweep with my gaze and spotted something at the foot of the sofa, near to where I had just been sitting. I went back into the room to investigate. It was a coin. I always leave my purse in my handbag in the locker, so it was unlikely the coin had rolled out of the open bum bag. In any case, when I picked it up I saw that it wasn't an English coin. It was about the size of a two pence piece, but silver in colour. There was a kind of shield with a trident shaped object on one face, and a '2' and a word that began with 'k' on the other. It was more evidence about the person who had been into the room and so I put it safely into my bum bag next to the red card.

# Chapter Twenty-two

On my way out of the hotel this afternoon I met Sanjay, one of the chefs, at reception. He was having a one-sided conversation with the receptionist and turned to me for help.

"Have you seen Poliakov?" he asked me.

"No, thank God." It was out before I could stop myself. But Sanjay's a nice lad with a good head on his shoulders and a sense of humour. He just smiled:

"Yeah, I know what you mean. He's creepy. I don't ever wanna get stuck in that back office with him, believe me. Maybe I should just leave a message for Mr Clark?"

"Why, what's up?"

"I don't know if I should talk about it here." He looked around at the foyer. Lev, the duty bellboy, was pacing and whistling, and eyeing up a group of 'ladies who lunch' who'd just spilled out of the restaurant. He seemed in a quandary, so I suggested:

"Shall we go and have a drink?" I indicated the bar.

"No, not in the hotel. It's kind of delicate," he said.

"Oh, Sanjay, you're not leaving, are you?"

"What?" he looked confused. "Wasn't planning to. You never know with Poliakov, though, do you?"

"What do you mean?" I was intrigued now and wanted to hear the rest. He hesitated a moment then asked:

"I'm having my break now. I need some air. Do you fancy walkin' somewhere? Not far."

"All right, I'm not going straight home today. Let's walk up to Town Hall Square."

We stepped outside, and he put his hands in his pockets and started off in a bouncing stride. When he saw I had difficulty keeping up he slowed down and said:

"You know who you always remind me of? My old English teacher, Mrs Wallace."

"Is that a good thing? Should I be flattered or insulted?"

"Nah, she was great," he was emphatic. "She was dead strict. Posh too and old-fashioned, like you."

"Thank you Sanjay."

"She was dead smart, though. You never messed with her cos she knew everythin' – there was no point pretendin' you'd forgotten your homework or couldn't do your coursework. She'd rip your head off if she caught you lyin.'"

"She sounds most attractive," I joked, but on the whole I was flattered by the comparison. Sanjay stopped, bringing me to a halt too, the better to make his real point:

"But I mean you could tell her anythin'. She never looked surprised or embarrassed or anythin', she just took it. You know what I mean? She was the first person I told that I wanted to do cooking – be a chef. And she told me it was a good choice because everybody needs to eat. Not like my dad. He wanted me to be a doctor," he laughed. "I got twenty-four percent in my biology mock exams. He was well gutted."

"Well you're an excellent chef now. He must be proud."

"Yeah," a lack of conviction. "He'll be pleased if I can get my own restaurant."

"What's this problem you needed to see Poliakov about

then?" I asked. We were turning towards the square, far enough from the hotel to be out of earshot.

"It's got to be Giorgio," he told me. "I mean I knew he was a real git, but I never thought he'd do somethin' like that."

"Like what?" I asked. "At the risk of sounding like your old English teacher too, you're not making yourself clear, Sanjay." He laughed:

"Yeah, you can do her voice too," he laughed and stared at me for a moment maybe wondering if I was Mrs Wallace in disguise. Then he went back to his concern. "I feel bad you see. He's let two people get the sack for thievin' when he's the one who's liftin' the stuff." I sat down on a bench opposite the Town Hall and invited him to join me. I was hoping to get some clarification of that last statement too.

"Who got the sack? And what has Giorgio been liftin'?"

"You remember the bellboy with the funny teeth, Alwin? He got sacked and so did Roxanne, the sous chef. They got the push for walkin' off with supplies from the kitchen." It didn't surprise me to hear that Alwin had been light-fingered. I didn't really know Roxanne, but I wondered if she'd fancied Alwin.

"Did Poliakov catch them?" I asked.

"No. We didn't catch no one. I told Poliakov that a few packets of things had gone missin' – coffee, sugar, stuff like that, and a few bits from the fridge. You know, you'd put left-over cream or smoked salmon and stuff in the fridge and when you came to use it the next day – vanished."

"But I don't understand why you thought it was Alwin and Roxanne that had stolen them. Lots of staff have access to the kitchen."

"I didn't give no names. I just told Poliakov the stuff

was missin'. Next thing I know, he's sacked 'em. I suspected Giorgio from day one."

"But how could he sack them without any proof?" The Bijou wasn't exempt from the employment laws.

"I don't know. He didn't tell me nothin'. But it wasn't them anyway. It has to be the Italian git, because the stuff's still walkin'." I couldn't understand why a chef would steal food. That made no sense either.

"Do you think he's selling it to someone?"

"No. It's not that much stuff. I don't know what he's nickin' it for." He paused to watch a podgy toddler who was chasing pigeons towards our bench, then said, "Unless he thinks he can drop me in it. Get me the sack. He'd like that." I thought about the marks on the carpets of the two suites.

"Are we talking about boxes of stuff, like this?" I made a vague measurement with my arms. "Heavy things?"

"Nah – just bits you could put in a pocket or a little backpack. Not worth takin' unless you was starving. Why do you ask?"

"Oh, I was just wondering how he would get them out of the hotel," I lied. "But if it's such a small amount why all the fuss?"

"That's Giorgio too. Says he don't want no thieves in his kitchen – get that, his kitchen." A thought came to him and he shared it with me. "Maybe he's bipolar or something. He nicks it but can't remember doing it." He stood up. "I've got to go to the bank," he explained. "Anyway, all I can do is tell Poliakov first before my mate Giorgio has the chance to finger me for it." I stood up too.

"Look, I've got an appointment to see Mr Clark. Do you want me to mention it to him?"

"Yeah, why not? It's his hotel. He should know." He turned to leave. "Oh yeah, and tell him I need a pay rise – or if not I'll settle for a one-way ticket to Alaska, for Giorgio. That should be just about far enough to send him."

# Chapter Twenty-three

I stayed in town after that and at about 3.45 set out for Ma Preston's. With every step I felt that I was going in the wrong direction. I didn't know how I would face Mr C. Presumably he would be dressed in his masculine attire today, but how could I stop myself superimposing the lilac eyeshadow and auburn wig? In my nervous state I'd probably get the giggles, make him angry and ruin everything. The main part of my mission, after all, was to persuade him to take seriously my evidence about Mr Poliakov, and the nearer I got to the tearooms, the less impressive that evidence seemed to me. Someone had been into two of the suites on my rounds and had used the bathroom and in one case removed a towel. He/she/they had stored something overnight on the carpet and had left behind a foreign coin. Mr Poliakov hadn't paid any attention to my report. He himself often went into the laundry room for no apparent reason. Someone had been stealing from the kitchen stores and Alwin and Roxanne had been sacked. Here rests the case for the prosecution.

Mr Clark was already there when I arrived, sitting in the Natalie corner. He was wearing an aubergine-coloured cord jacket and dark trousers. He had lost the vulnerability of yesterday evening. Today he seemed guarded, wary but prepared to be firm. He got up as I approached and so focused was he on me that, on standing up, he backed into a waitress and received half the sickly buttercream of a pistachio cupcake on the sleeve of his jacket. Lots of apologies, some dabbing at the material then the jacket was stripped off and taken away by the waitress for sponging. I took advantage of the diversion to sit down and take an inventory of all my limbs. All present and in the correct positions. In an effort to show composure, I started to talk before he had a chance to say anything:

"I can't tell you how sorry I am about bursting in on you yesterday evening. It wasn't my intention to invade your privacy. And I'm sorry for laughing the way I did. I was embarrassed. I wasn't laughing at you, I promise." The brown eyes, minus mascara and eyeshadow, were weighing me up. But he didn't respond to my apology. Instead he asked:

"What will you have, Miss Baxter? I'm going to have scones with jam and cream. Will you keep me company? I hope your slim figure doesn't mean you're one of those ladies perpetually on a diet?" Professional charm. 'He could bottle it and sell it at Harrods' I thought, and kicked myself for having made such a clumsy opening. He ordered tea and scones for two and when the waitress had gone he began:

"The fault was entirely mine yesterday evening for opening the door without first ascertaining that the person outside was the one I expected. But I accept your apology for the laughter. I must admit I find the derision hard to take, even after all these years, although I should be used to it by now." The ghost of yesterday's anger flitted across his eyes as he continued to appraise me. I felt like a fourteen-year-old up before the Head for giggling in assembly. His jacket was returned and he arranged it on the back of his chair before turning to ask me:

"And how many people have you already told?" He uses that same trick on TV. The quick upward glance, eyes just glinting from under half-closed lids. It throws the interviewee off-balance and often gets the truth out of the villains or puts them at least on the defensive. I was proud and relieved not to have to defend myself.

"No one," I answered and held his gaze as he frisked me with his own personal lie detector. "I've spoken to Phil Riley, but of course he already knows." He gave me the impression that I had passed the test. He dropped his gaze, looked momentarily out into the courtyard, then returned to the fight with that same stabbing look directed at me from semi-closed eyes.

"And how much are you asking for your continued silence?"

That was a slap I hadn't expected. I was glad I was sitting down. Glad also that the super-efficient waitress chose that moment to arrive with the tea and scones, placing teapot and plates on the table. Mr Clark began to pour the tea and that gave me a few moments to try to master the succession of different emotions that his question had produced. Blackmailing Mr C had never occurred to me and why would it have? Selling the story to a newspaper, yes. It was a simple transaction: an exchange of goods. Blackmail was disgusting and illegal and sick. Shock, self-righteous indignation, venality, indecision popped up as possible responses, like multiple-choice answers in a TV quiz. Which one would I choose?

"There's a microphone hidden somewhere, isn't there?"

I asked. "I've watched your programme. I know your tricks." I raised my newly poured tea to my lips. I didn't quite have my little finger crooked as I lifted the china cup, but I wanted to show that I was calm, worldly, mistress of this tense situation. The hot tea scalded my tongue and I hastily put down the cup, spilling tea in my saucer, image dented. He waited patiently for my answer, confident, I could see, that whatever I said he had his deckchair parked on the moral high ground. Well I'd show him I had a soupçon of integrity, whatever he thought. I could give only one reply to such a question:

"My silence can't be bought," I told him, "it can only be freely given, and I give it." He looked unconvinced of my sincerity and said nothing. My scalded tongue smarted. My mother used to say, "Liars have a permanent sore tip at the end of their tongue." The memory of her disapproving look drove me to confess. "I was tempted. I actually had a plan to ring up one of the newspapers and try to sell them the story." He smirked. I could see that my confession fitted his concept of human nature better than my previous altruism.

"But you obviously didn't have any evidence," he concluded. "It would have been your word against mine."

"I'll have you know I'm well known for telling the truth," I protested.

"So am I," he answered, and this gentle reminder of his whiter-than-white reputation nationwide made us both laugh. My next question was out of my mouth before my brain could censor it:

"Then why don't you? I mean why don't you tell the truth about your – I don't know what to call it – your hobby? Why aren't you honest about that, too?"

"You haven't touched your scones," he replied. "Try them with some of this jam." He spooned some strawberry jam onto my plate and waited whilst I tasted it. "I think you already know the answer to that question. After all, you thought you had a story to sell." I received the hard stare straight to camera at this point. "Which paper were you going to try first, by the way?"

"The *Mail*."

"Bull's eye." He surveyed me again as if really seeing me for the first time. "Natalie said you were wasted in housekeeping. What's your background, Miss Baxter?" I hadn't come prepared for an interview but I managed to condense my working life into a couple of sentences. As he listened, some of his *Today Programme* abrasiveness began to leave him. He remarked:

"My mother bought my first pair of long trousers at Grearson's, on the never-never. But that was before your time."

"That depends how recently you got your first long trousers," I answered. He chuckled at that one.

"But why housekeeping at the Bijou?"

"It is all I have been offered since Grearson's folded. In case you hadn't noticed, we're in a recession and I am over fifty. I'm also single and trying to hold up a house that's falling down around my ears. I was desperate."

"So desperate, you might still sell my secret in the future. How do I know I can trust you?" he asked.

"Trust, I don't know. But you said yourself I have no evidence."

"People might still believe you. The *Mail* might well." He poured more hot water into the pot and topped up my cup.

"A lifelong bachelor always provokes hostility and suspicion in some parts of the press."

"Then perhaps it's time to get married?" I suggested and felt my face begin to burn as I became aware of what I'd just said to my boss. But he laughed, a real booming laugh that made a few people turn to look.

"You're the first woman who's ever asked me," he confided.

"But I didn't, I never meant… " I blabbered. The temperature in the room was suddenly in the nineties.

"My little joke," he reassured me. "But seriously, Miss Baxter, do you give me your word that you won't talk to the press or anyone else about how I spend my free evenings?"

"I already gave you my word, but I'll give it again. And I keep my promises." He scrutinised me as he drank his tea then gave his verdict:

"My gut instinct tells me you're honest, and I always follow my gut – in more ways than one." He laughed and patted the spare flesh where his waist should have been. "I don't promise anything, and this is in no way a bribe to buy your silence, but I'll have a word with Poliakov. First chance we get, we'll move you to something more suited to your talents."

I think I'd half expected the sack to be the outcome of my tea with Mr C and I was too dazed by this turn of events to even thank him. Instead I began to rattle through what I'd also come to explain to him: Poliakov's strange behaviour, the rooms that had been disturbed, the missing supplies. I laid my evidence on the table.

"Cyrillic script," he said, examining the card. "Russian. It's probably Poliakov's. Have you asked him?" Nothing so simple had crossed my mind. I shook my head weakly. "How about phoning the number?" Another feeble shake of the head. I'd keep Mrs A's ghosts to myself for now. He already thought I was pathetic. He pulled out his phone and jabbed in the numbers. After a pause I heard him say:

"This is Marc Clark. I'd be grateful if you'd get back to me. It's in connection with something found in the laundry room of the Bijou Hotel. Thanks." He put the card down. "We'll see what that produces." Then he picked up the coin. "This is Ukrainian. Have we had any Ukrainian guests?"

"No one has stayed in that room since I cleaned it."

"Perhaps you overlooked the coin. Cleaning must be tiring work."

"I'm very thorough."

"I'm sure you are." He pocketed his phone and my exhibits for the prosecution. Time to move on. "Thank you for raising these concerns and the problems in the kitchen. Poliakov certainly hasn't mentioned these problems to us, but then we pay him to manage. I will certainly follow them up. But look, I'm off to the States for a few days – important contract to discuss – so I'm pretty well tied up for now. Leave it with me. I'll check in again with you when I get back." The waitress responded instantly to his call for the bill. "In the meantime," he stood up and helped me on with my jacket, "I'd be grateful if you'd keep up your vigilance at the hotel, and above all, I shall trust you to keep mum." Did I imagine the wink?

# Chapter Twenty-four

"What will you have, Pru?" Phil was haunting the doorway of the snug when I arrived on Thursday evening. He looked as if he hadn't slept for a week.

"Drinks are on me," I told him. "I've just been given promotion." At least I thought I had. Poliakov hadn't seemed very convinced when he told me. He had stopped me as I was on my way out of the foyer. Joyful or congratulatory he was not.

"Next month you work in office, Mr Clark say," he'd said, as if he were telling me his cat had just been run over. I hadn't suspected a capacity for such deep emotions in him. He clearly didn't fancy sharing his office with me any more than I wanted to work beside him. I couldn't believe Mr C had responded so quickly. In order to convince myself of my sudden vertiginous elevation to the heights of office work, as from next month, I had to blurt it out to Phil. But Phil was too preoccupied to register my news and only said:

"Good for you, so it's my treat."

We settled ourselves with our drinks in the corner opposite the door, the better to spy intruders. The RATS often came in here for a drink, but usually only after rehearsal. Phil was convinced, however, that the group had its closet alcoholics and was terrified that Sheila might prove to be one of them this evening. Our secret rendezvous would be hard to explain to her given our past 'form' in her eyes.

"I had no idea you and Mr Clark were such good friends," I accused.

"I want you to know that Marc and I are just friends. We share the same hobby. Don't get the idea that there's anything going on between us. I mean I'm not gay." He took a large swig of his G and T. "We were at school together. All the council estate boys stuck together at first. We've kept in touch since school. We usually meet up when he's in town. It's one of the few occasions I get to, well, dress up. In fact," he cleared his throat and fidgeted on the settle beside me, "this dressing business started at school. Well, it did for me."

"I don't know if you should tell me any details if it's about Mr C too."

"Boys' school," he went on, disregarding me. "When we did plays, Shakespeare, anything, I got to be the girl. I was good at it. I enjoyed it."

"So Donna Lucia isn't your first?" He continued to ignore me.

"I'm not gay," he repeated. "I don't fancy men, even when they're dressed as women, funnily enough. I just like the way I feel in skirts and soft fabrics. I love the shoes, the colours, the choice. I've always loved shopping with Sheila."

"Most men hate it," I said. "Didn't Sheila ever comment?"

"She appreciates my taste. I choose most of her clothes. I know better than she does what suits her." Sheila was always very well dressed. Now I knew her secret.

"You know it's not fair. You women are always banging on about equality. But you can wear what you like. You can wear trousers, even a shirt and tie, and no one calls you a dyke.

Why can't men have the same freedom? Why shouldn't I go to work in high-heeled boots and a leather skirt?" I couldn't stop myself:

"You haven't got the hips, Phil. You'd look like a chocolate bar that had shrunk in the wrapper. And you're rubbish at walking in high heels. It's like watching a two-legged earthquake." He registered this criticism. "Phil, I'm all for equality and liberation. As far as I'm concerned, you can go to work in a pink tutu, if you want – though pink's not really your colour – but, let's face it, you've no chance of striking a blow for freedom of choice when you're too 'frit' to even tell the truth to your own wife." The freedom fighter faltered and turned slowly back into Phil. He sighed:

"You've never been married, Pru." I waited for the 'lucky you' that always seems to follow that statement, the put-down that pretends to praise my good sense in avoiding the net, but it didn't come. Instead he said; "Next year will be our thirtieth anniversary. I can't imagine life without Sheila. I know I should have told her when we first met, but I thought I'd given it up for good then. I can't tell her now. You don't know her, Pru. Well," he corrected himself, "obviously you do, but you're not married to her. She'd have my balls for hiding things from her for all these years, then she'd walk out." He jumped up to go for a refill. I'd barely touched my drink. "I need another of these, Pru. How about you?" I shook my head. When he came back I said:

"Logically, Phil, you have to make a choice: Sheila or skirts." He considered this for a moment, then gave me a wide smile.

"Look here, Pru, as I see it you're the fly in the ointment, so to speak. A lovely fly, don't get me wrong, but I don't see the need to make a choice. It's not like I'm having an affair. It's completely harmless, and it's not even as if I do it every day. Sheila knows nothing. She's happy. I'm happy." He looked very pleased with himself at that moment. "The only one unhappy is you."

"No, Phil. If I hated Sheila I might be able to agree to keep her in the dark and have a good laugh about it, but I don't hate her. She's my best friend. I won't lie to her, Phil." He took another swig from his glass. "I won't tell her either, but you have to." He faced this thought a moment then went into negotiation mode:

"Look at it this way, Pru. What does she gain by knowing?"

"The truth." He didn't think much of my logic.

"I'll grant you, she gets the truth, but if it makes her unhappy, where's the sense in that?"

Did I want Sheila to be unhappy? It was a fair question. What could it matter to me if she had a slanted view of her husband, if there were a few pixels I could see that never came into focus for her? What did I know about the secrets and lies of long-term marrieds? More importantly for me, what was my motive? Was I so intent on the truth because I felt it was her right, or because I wanted to throw a bomb into her perfect relationship and watch it disintegrate?

There was something unpleasant at the heart of my dilemma and I was being forced to recognise and confront it. It was power. I'd never had power before – real power over the lives of other people. With a word in the right place I had the power still to destroy Mr C's career, or raise a storm in Phil and Sheila's marriage. For a moment, the sense of holding those people and their future in my hands gave me a dizzying sense of elation, but only for a moment. Then I realised that I too was 'frit'. I wanted Phil to tell the truth. I needed him to tell the truth in order to take away my power over him and his marriage. Power needed strength to wield it and strength to contain it. I was not absolutely convinced that I might not – in a moment of pain or foot-in-mouth stupidity – give in to the temptation and use that power out of weakness.

Phil sensed he was winning the argument. I was silent, thinking for so long. He looked so pathetically grateful that I had the urge to employ a Marc Clark tactic – the darted look from under half-closed eyelids, and the killer question:

"How do you know you can trust me not to tell her?" Let him see the venom, the jealousy, the vile, black discontent with my disappointing life that I kept hidden from everyone, even from myself. Let him see all your possibilities, Pru. Let him really understand who you are, what disillusion can drive you to. I wavered, but of course I didn't. I said:

"Let me think about it. I won't say anything to Sheila. You know I'm not like that. But I really wish you would tell her." The usual, wishy-washy, lukewarm Pru, then?

# Chapter Twenty-five

I kept out of Poliakov's way even more than usual after he had grudgingly told me about my promotion. I decided not to mention anything to Mrs A. Although I was sure Mr Clark wanted me to work as office manager I was equally sure that neither Poliakov nor I could picture ourselves together in that office. In fact the thought of sharing a closed space with the unsmiling Napoleon took all the edge off my leaving housekeeping and made me wonder if I wouldn't rather carry on hoovering. Just that thought was on my mind this morning when he caught me. I was wheeling out my trolley from the service room when he appeared from behind the laundry skip. He'd waited until Mrs A was out of the way, then just materialised. For once, I was the one who got the shock.

"You give this Clark?" He flourished the red card with the Cyrillic script. No preliminaries, straight to the point.

"Yes, I found it on my trolley."

"Why you give Clark?"

"Sorry?"

"Why you not give me?" The truth was of course that I trusted Mr Clark and I didn't trust him any further than I could spit a grape pit. But I couldn't tell him that, so I resorted to the time-honoured excuse of the gormless Grearson's packer.

"I didn't think."

"You make me trouble. Big trouble." Those dead eyes were sparkling for once, but there was no joy behind them.

"I'm sorry, Mr Poliakov. But it's just a card. I don't understand why you think you're in trouble over a card." It was only a card, not a packet of white powder. Why should he be so angry? He said nothing. His silence was unnerving. I had no idea whether he was going to laugh it off or explode. "Look," I said, trying to mask my disquiet, "I took it to Mr Clark because of the letter he sent to us. Next time if I find something, I'll bring it to you." That was a lie but it also seemed to me to serve as an adequate apology and I didn't see any need to prolong the conversation. I gave my trolley a tug to be on my way. It was blocked. He had caught hold of it and wasn't about to let go.

"Sorry, Mr Poliakov, but I have my work to do. We're very busy what with the Richard III exhibition and everything." He still held on.

"No next time. You work, you not look. You not find. Is all. I also make big trouble." The quietness of his voice, I had to strain to hear it, didn't mask the menace behind it. A spark of anger came to me from the old Pru, scourge of the packers. It was an instinct of self-defence too. He was holding back the trolley, would he grab me next? And no one to hear me if I screamed.

"Is that some kind of threat?" I asked keeping my voice as steady as I could. In reply, he laughed, a quick 'ha' of expelled breath. I'd never seen him so much as smile before. The laugh was infinitely more chilling than the dead-eyed stare. Then he pushed the trolley suddenly towards me, aiming a kick at the wheel nearest him.

"You work," he said, and watched me as I backed out of the door.

I went around for the rest of the morning 'watching my back'. He'd said nothing really intimidating but still I felt uncomfortable. How would I manage when I had to work in the same office as him? After this exchange I made up my mind that it would be better to carry on changing duvet covers than to have that reptilian stare freezing my liver every day. I would write Mr C a note for when he returned.

I had brought my car, the old Volvo tank, as I usually do on Fridays when I do my supermarket raid after work. Other days I leave it at home and take the bus because parking is difficult. We're not allowed to park at the front of the hotel, and the garage parking is for guests' cars. We staff have to look for a space in the overflow car park at the back. You have to enter a code to get the barrier to lift, so you have to park on double yellow lines in order to run in and get the day's code from reception and register your car, then race back and hope that the code opens the barrier. It's a performance I can only allow myself once a week.

When I came out of work at 2.45, I got into the car and was congratulating myself on the fact that I hadn't seen Ivan for the rest of the morning and thinking that maybe he'd got over his tantrum. But I'd still have to turn down that promotion, damn him. I switched on the engine, put the car into first gear and couldn't work out why it wouldn't go forwards. The steering felt as if it were locked. I got out to see if I'd been clamped or if there was something blocking the wheels. There was: four flat tyres. I walked all the way round kicking each wheel in turn, and wondering if I were suffering from early-onset dementia – seeing things that weren't really there. How was it possible to have four flat tyres all at once? I was paralysed for a moment by the suspicion that connected this discovery with my earlier conversation with Poliakov. 'I make big trouble,' he'd said. Letting the air out of my tyres was the kind of low trick a mean-spirited little runt like him would think of pulling. I went in search of a witness to confirm for me the sinister reality.

I looked for Dave as the only person still around that I trusted. I found him lurking in the boiler room with a copy of yesterday's *Sun*.

"Worall four?"

"Flat as pancakes."

"Bin drivin' uver tin tacks?"

"They were fine this morning. Someone's let the air out."

"I'll get the air machine. Soon 'ave yer rollin'." At that point I was convinced that the tyres had just been deflated, so I felt rather bad that Dave had the bother of unearthing the air machine and then carrying it out to the car park, because he of course saw at once what I'd missed.

"Airs no bledy good. The've bin slashed, cut, look." On the nearside front I could now see a long rent in the rubber of the tyre. "Nearly bald these're. Good job you weren't stopped." Dave seemed to think a Good Samaritan had done me a favour. He was probably wondering too what sort of shady characters I knew and what I could have done to provoke such an attack.

"But who, why?" I couldn't seem to get more words out. It was a rhetorical question in any case. I knew who and why but I didn't dare verbalise it. I looked around. Poliakov was sure to be hidden somewhere enjoying my confusion, my sense of being menaced.

"There's sum right bledy mental cases knockin' round. Half the young-uns are on summat. Cumon we'll see if Ivan's gorra picture forrus on 'is telly."

Poliakov wasn't there. Of course he wouldn't be. Linda, yet another young, vapid receptionist finally managed to get the CCTV footage going. No one suspicious, and no one at all near my car. But the camera had been switched off more than half the morning.

"Call the police?" I asked Dave.

"Norra lot they can do for ya. The telly were switched off. Unless it's for insurance."

"I've only got third party."

"That's a bugger."

Dave had a mate. A phone call, some haggling about prices and at least the practical problem of how to get the car out of the car park and eventually 'rollin' again was resolved. I got the bus home and forgot about the shopping. The problem of how to pay for a breakdown lorry and four new tyres I could wrestle with later. It wasn't the cost that worried me. Money was already pouring out of my account just as if the bank had been hit by a US drone. It was the thought that someone with a very sharp knife had chosen to do harm, and had deliberately targeted my property. I received the message loud and clear: if we can do this to your car in a public place in broad daylight…

I couldn't finish that thought on the bus home. I was heading back to a large, silent house where I would be sleeping, or trying to, all night alone. I did try out other ideas. It was possibly some anti-Swedish maniac, or a disillusioned Volvo owner, or even some character I cut up at a roundabout, who had practised his whittling skills on my tyres. But I knew that was all nonsense. It was Poliakov. He didn't do it himself. He's far too devious for that. But he knows people who will do that for him. What else might they do for him? That was not a question to be asking myself, I decided; better to concentrate on why he had it done. This was no manager of a hotel but someone engaged in an activity, centred on the hotel, that he needed to protect by threats and intimidation. Whatever he was up to must involve large sums of money to be so vital to him and I wasn't sure how far he would go to protect it. I'd promised Mr C to keep up my vigilance but I was beginning to think that it might be better and safer to become one of Mrs A's wise monkeys and look for a new job.

# Chapter Twenty-six

I needed a lift. All the book club women were going to Moira's favourite restaurant out at Bradgate to celebrate her birthday. We'd clubbed together to buy her a package at Ragdale Hall spa as a present. I felt like stealing the envelope. My nerves had more need of calming than Moira's. I told Sheila what had happened to my car because I had to ask her for a lift and also because she could see when she picked me up that I was preoccupied. But I also told her to keep it quiet, at least for this evening. I didn't want to go spoiling Moira's party. I should, of course, have known Sheila better.

The food was lovely, everyone said. I don't remember what I ordered and I couldn't tell you what I ate. I just chewed away like an old tortoise finding my thoughts sauntering down the path I'd forbidden them to take. The others were into their favourite topic of conversation – how useless their men are. They were swapping stories of their exasperating ways. Not having a man in my life, I couldn't contribute and so I took my thoughts for a walk in another territory. I was wondering if I'd ever felt threatened before and instantly thought of Geoffrey. But then I thought he didn't count. He certainly hated me, but that was natural somehow and not my fault. I'd annoyed him just by being born. But I couldn't think of a time when I'd ever given anyone reason to hate me – or at least hate me enough to want to do me physical damage. Not until now.

"Pru's quiet tonight," Liz Bembridge commented.

"She's lucky. She's an independent woman," said Moira.

"I'll bet her sitting room wasn't stinking of beer last Saturday, like mine was. Mike had six of his mates over – grown men behaving like kids swearing at rugby players in New Zealand," said Beverley.

"We had Katie's new in-laws round and some of the plaster that Tony, the DIY baron, put up two weeks ago came down – all over the dinner table. I told him all along it was a job for a professional."

"Oh no, Joy, I hope you weren't still eating," Moira said.

"Chocolate mousse made with eight eggs. Had to throw it all away and give them yoghurt."

"She's had her tyres slashed," said Sheila.

"Sheila, I asked you not to… " I started.

"What?" said Moira.

"Where?" asked Joy.

"At the hotel where she works," Sheila answered. So of course I then had to tell them all what had happened and the party atmosphere spluttered out before we'd even got to the cake.

Liz thought she'd console me:

"You know it's almost every weekend now that there's a burnt-out car in the hedgerow where I walk Byron."

"There are such thugs about. All they want to do is destroy things," Beverley agreed.

"It wasn't random," I put her straight. "I was targeted by my boss at the hotel." I wish I could have captured the next sequence on film for an acting workshop. All my friends' faces were showing different degrees of the same concerned expression, whilst their eyes were all asking, 'My God, has she finally lost it?' I told them about the threats he'd made in the morning.

"Go to the police," Liz insisted.

"She's got no proof," Sheila pointed out.

"I have no witnesses," I confirmed. "It's my word against his."

"Well I know who I'd believe," said Joy.

"But you're not the police," Sheila reminded her.

"But even they can see what a creep he is," said Moira. "I remember him from the party at the hotel. Detestable man."

"They can't arrest people just for being creeps," said Beverley.

"Pity," said Sheila. "It would save a lot of money spent on divorces."

"What about Mr Clark? What does he have to say?" asked Moira.

"He doesn't know. He's in the States right now." Silence. We'd got to a dead end.

"Well you can't go back to work there, Pru. You'll have to resign." Moira had solved my problem.

"And do what? You do remember how long it took me to get this job?"

"But if you're not safe there," said Joy. Another dead end. Everyone felt compelled to find a solution to my problem but couldn't conjure one up, hard as they tried. I felt guilty at having presented them with a dilemma they couldn't fix. We were saved from our frustration when a large, pale-lemon, frosted confection, ablaze with candles and sparklers, was paraded in and we all struggled back into our festive mood to sing 'Happy Birthday' to Moira.

After we'd said our goodbyes to the others in the restaurant car park Moira said:

"I don't like to think of you going to work there tomorrow, Pru."

"I hate the thought of working there any day," I said. "But needs must."

"Would you like me to ask Matt to come along with you?"

"Good at hoovering is he?" said Sheila. "Send him round to my house then."

"Oh Sheila, this is no laughing matter. Pru's been threatened. I just think it might be a good idea for a man to talk to this creepy Russian. He obviously thinks he can walk all over Pru. Maybe Phil and Matt could both go." The image of mild, bespectacled Matt and cuddly, cross-dressing Phil attempting to intimidate ice-man Poliakov almost prompted a smile from me. Even if he understood their English, and with Matt's convolutions that was always an art, he'd find their physical menace risible – except that Ivan never laughed.

"I appreciate your concern for me, Moira, but I think all I can do is keep a low profile until Mr Clark returns."

In the car Sheila and I talked about other things. There were details to be finalised about the charity opening performance of *Charley's Aunt* that Sheila needed me to take care of, and we discussed ways of publicising the event. At the roundabout on the ring road Sheila asked:

"Are you sure you wouldn't like to come and stay with us tonight?" It was attractive, the idea of being in a house where I felt protected. Sheila drove round the roundabout as I came to a decision.

"If I stay with you tonight," I said, "I'm not sure I'll ever be able to go home. I can't afford to start that – being afraid to be alone – not at my age." She didn't argue for once but she watched until I had gone into the house and switched the lights on, downstairs and up, before she drove off.

# Chapter Twenty-seven

In 1995 we had a strike at Grearson's. It lasted two weeks. That was the only time in my life when I was conscious of being a figure of hate. How could I not be conscious of it when every day I had to cross the packers' picket line? The first day when I had to drive through the crowd of women with their placards, was really frightening. They had stopped the car and started to argue with me to convince me not to cross the line. When I had started to drive on they had called me a scab and worse. I remember them saying I'd get what was coming to me and wondering just what they had in mind. As long as they were shouting I felt strong, but as soon as I got inside into the unnaturally quiet building, I'd had to sit down to get my shaking limbs under control. Mr Grearson saw what a state I was in:

"I'm going to call the police," he said. I had enough of my faculties back by then to stop him.

"They're not doing anything illegal. It's their right to picket peacefully, as they're doing. If they try and stop delivery lorries, then will be the time to act."

"But you can't go through that every morning just to get to work. Why not come in with me tomorrow? We can agree a convenient pick-up point." It was a tempting offer. We'd both be stronger if we arrived together, and the girls would be more guarded with the boss. But I turned him down.

"They are not going to intimidate me into doing anything different," I said. "I'm not going to let them win. If they see they've scared me I'll never be able to work with them in the future."

"I might have to sack the lot of them anyway," Mr Grearson risked a look out of the window, "or at least the ringleaders like that McCrae woman."

"I'm sure it won't come to that," I said. I thought it would be a two-day wonder, a chance to let off steam and enjoy the fine weather. I was wrong. They were striking to persuade Mr Grearson to reinstate a young Asian girl who they said had been discriminated against. She was a girl who'd never managed a five-day week in the ten months she'd been there, and had been late on almost all of the mornings she had managed to get herself to work. All the disciplinary procedures had been followed before dismissal. I couldn't understand why the union was supporting her. Shona McCrae, the union rep, had somehow convinced them that we were operating a closed shop, even though we had the evidence to prove that we weren't.

At the beginning of the second week, the picket line was getting thin and Shona had to bring in reinforcements, men as well as women. They stopped the car as usual, although I didn't see the point in this. If they hadn't convinced me to stay outside once in the previous week, what new arguments could they bring? One of the men held a placard saying, 'Grearson racist!' in large red painted letters. He stomped the end of the wooden pole on the bonnet of my car to make sure I read the message. The Volvo was quite new then. I switched off the engine and got out of the car to see if it had been damaged. There was of course no dent: it's a tank on wheels. But I still challenged him.

"You realise you risk being charged with criminal damage if you interfere with any vehicle entering the premises?" I asked.

"And you realise you're collaborating with a racist?" he retorted, mocking my 'posh' accent.

"And calling Mr Grearson a racist is slander," I said, "in front of witnesses too." Shona was suddenly at my elbow.

"That's his pet parrot," she said. "You won't get anything out of her except what he's taught her to say."

"Well," I said, " if you'll just get out of the way, I'll be getting back to my cage, and crack open a few sunflower seeds." The man laughed at that and so did a few of the women, but not Shona.

"Think you're so bloody clever, don't you," she said, "cos you went to a snobby school and can speak proper English?"

"No, I don't," I said. "I don't think that, Shona. That's what you think." I got back into the car and prepared to drive off. Shona threw a half-hearted 'scab' after me and hung around by the car door even after the others had moved. "You know what puzzles me, Shona?" I looked up at her face divided in two by the half-open window of my car. "How do you get dressed in the morning with that great big chip on your shoulder?" In the wing mirror I saw the up-turned two fingers but there was a tiredness in the gesture and I suddenly felt sorry for her.

Once the strike had caved in and everyone was back at work, Shona quietened down. We made an unspoken agreement to avoid each other as much as possible, and managed to uphold it for most of the next thirteen years. It was the collapse of Grearson's that finally brought us together. All the staff walked out on the last day in a group, Shona and I brought up the rear. It was the first and last time we walked into the car park side by side, although we've probably remained together ever since as consecutive numbers in the unemployment statistics.

# Chapter Twenty-eight

Going into the Bijou today, I must admit I was not so much scared as apprehensive – a new feeling for me, and one that I didn't like. I decided that the only way to overcome it was to tackle it head on. Poliakov was no Shona and I had no Mr Grearson to watch my back, but the speed and violence of Poliakov's reaction had unnerved me and I had to react at once, or live in fear. The devious, underhand way he'd gone about damaging my property and intimidating me, made me blaze with anger. He was the last person I wanted to see and at the same time the very person I knew I had to confront.

He wasn't there when I arrived. He was 'unavailable' – a new word for the receptionist – when I went to seek him out in my break. The thought crossed my mind that he was maybe avoiding me – avoiding a confrontation. Was he 'frit'? That was a comforting thought. I finally cornered him as I was about to leave. He was at the reception desk as I was handing in my work card and that day's key card at the end of my shift.

"Mr Poliakov, I'd like to speak to you, please. It's very urgent." He didn't, as I'd half expected, flap at me to go away and turn on his heel. Instead he stared at a point somewhere over my left shoulder in an effort to look like he was listening.

"It's about my car," I went on, "and I'd like to speak in

private." Before he could stop me, or more to the point, before I could lose my nerve, I'd skipped behind reception and into the back office.

Sanjay's comment about not getting stuck in the office with him came to mind, but it was too late now, and in any case I was probably the wrong sex to need to worry on that score. It was my first time in the back office and I discovered it was very neat. Mrs A cleaned it, under Poliakov's supervision, and the gleaming, polished laminate of the desk was a credit to her elbow grease. The only things on the surface of the desk were a telephone and the desktop computer. Poliakov, who had slipped in behind me, hurriedly turned the screen off. The spreadsheet I'd glimpsed obviously had something on it he didn't want made public.

"I want to make a complaint about damage to my car when it was in the overflow car park yesterday." I plonked myself down on a chair in case he had any thoughts of shooing me out quickly.

"Your car," he repeated. He stayed standing. "There was crash?" I fought back the urge to say –'don't play the innocent with me. You know perfectly well what happened. You arranged it.' Instead I countered his faked innocence with my own:

"No, Mr. Poliakov, not a crash – criminal damage. Someone came into the car park and slashed – cut with a knife – all the tyres on my car." The advantage of having soulless eyes like Poliakov's, I realised, is that you don't have to change expression when something surprises you – or pretend to be surprised when something doesn't.

"Someone outside come in the car park?"

"Yes. Apparently."

“Is not responsible the hotel. There is sign say this.”

“I know there’s a disclaimer in the car park. But I think the least you can do is to make an official report to the hotel owners, and give a warning to all the guests that there’s a knife-wielding maniac on the loose.” I’d lost him, as I’d intended. I pulled my ready-prepared report out of my bag and placed it neatly on the desk facing him. “I’ve written and signed the report so there’s no need for you to do anything except make copies for Mr Clark and Mr Strutt.” He prodded the report with his index finger as if it were a dirty handkerchief soiling his pristine desk. But he still said nothing.

“If you like, I can write you a warning for the guests about the car park. I can put it straight onto the hotel message system. I’m quite good with computers.” I got up to move around the desk and take charge of the keyboard. He blocked my way. He’s not tall or well built, but he’s fast and he has a kind of force field around him that pulls you up short.

“No,” he said. “Message to guests is not necessary. Was not guest car. Only your car.” There was a little smile that came with the words, ‘your car’. I wanted to slap him. He thought he was so clever. Instead I asked:

“Why do you think it was only my car?” All the response I got was an elaborate shrug. There might be a million reasons why someone would hate me, it suggested. And then:

“Is possible you make somebody angry – piss him off.”

“And why was the CCTV switched off when it happened?”

“Electric problem. Now is fixed.” I knew already that no problem had been reported to Dave. ‘Yes,’ I thought, ‘now is fixed, you think. But just wait till I start working in here. Then we’ll see who gets fixed.’ I decided to remind him:

“The first of the month is next week,” I said. “When I

start working in here I'll need a desk too. Where shall we put it?" I looked across to the other side of the room. "Over there in that corner?" I wouldn't have noticed them if I hadn't come round to take charge of the computer. On top of the low cupboard that ran the length of the far wall, were three rolled-up sleeping bags and a rucksack. We had a luggage store in the hotel, as Natalie had found out. And Mr Poliakov knew where it was. He had shown her. There was no reason for those items to be in the manager's office. Just visible in the rucksack, where one of the straps wasn't properly closed, was a box of tea bags, just like the ones I use to refill the tea-and coffee-making facilities in the guest suites. I knew Poliakov was watching me as I registered first surprise and then a sudden understanding. The shapes I'd seen on the carpet of the Valkyrie and Tannhauser suites, the disappearance of small quantities of supplies from the kitchen stores now made sense. I thought I'd better make a comment, so I said:

"Planning on doing some camping, are you, Mr. Poliakov?" With hindsight I wish I hadn't said that because it was probably that flash of recognition that pushed him to really stitch me up.

# Chapter Twenty-Nine

Two days later I was called down to reception and asked by a young girl dressed as a policewoman if I would mind opening my locker and having the contents inspected. She explained that one of the guests had reported losing an item that morning, and she and her colleague had been called to carry out a thorough search of the hotel. I told her I wouldn't dream of not cooperating with the police. I didn't like the thought of thieves operating in the hotel. I took the key from the front pocket of my bum bag, opened up the door of the locker and stepped back to let her carry out her search. Even though I knew it would be fruitless, it was good to have a few minutes distraction from pushing the hoover. She rummaged for a few seconds and then brought out a pink and grey plastic purse with a sequin and rhinestone heart on the front.

"Is this yours, madam?" she asked. 'You must be joking,' I thought, 'I've got taste.' Then the significance of her discovery hit me full in the stomach.

"No," I said. "I've never seen it before."

"Is this the missing item?" she asked Poliakov. He nodded and did his best to give me a look that spoke of betrayal of trust and profound disappointment. Mrs A, whose locker had been the next on the search list, clasped my arm in solidarity, but her eyes unmistakably said:

'I warned you he was dangerous.'

*

"And you've no idea how the purse came to be in your locker?" the detective constable asked.

"None at all," I answered. I was interviewed this morning, under caution by the police.

"Could you have left the locker open at any time yesterday?"

"No. I always put my handbag in there so I make absolutely sure that I shut the door. It locks automatically."

"And as I understand it, the locker can only be opened by your key?"

"Yes."

"Then perhaps you left your key somewhere unattended. Someone might have taken it, even for a few moments."

"No I keep it in my bum bag around my waist. It never leaves me all morning."

"Do you take the key home with you? Could someone have taken it from your car or your house?"

"My car's just come back from the mechanic's. And there is no one at home."

I'd never seen the inside of a police station before, and I felt very dirty sitting there. I think it was the crowning humiliation of my life – if crowns and humiliation can go together. Sheila came with me. She and Phil have been so kind. Of course they know I'm innocent because they know all about Poliakov – I've told them everything that I had told

Mr C and about seeing the stuff in the office. When I was telling them, it sounded logical, convincing. When I told the police it sounded as if I were trying to lay the blame on someone else. But I didn't take that purse. They tell me it was stuffed with cash and credit cards, and it's true I've got some big bills to pay, but I'd never dream of stealing to save myself. And even if I could have got up the courage and smothered my basic instincts, I wouldn't have been stupid enough to steal from a guest. Poliakov just had to find a way to keep me out of that office.

"Miss Baxter, you're telling me that when you left the Lohengrin Suite yesterday after cleaning it you did not have Miss Liashenko's purse with you?"

"Certainly, I did not."

"Yet when you opened your locker during the search being carried out by our officers, the purse was inside?"

"Yes, I told you."

"But you see my problem, Miss Baxter? You tell me you never saw the purse until you found it in your locker, and yet the information about how the locker operates suggests that only you could have put it there."

"Unless there was a duplicate key. That's what he wants you to think, but don't you see that he could have had a copy of the key made, just to set me up?"

"Who?"

"Poliakov, the manager of course."

"So you are suggesting the manager of the hotel stole the guest's purse?"

"Yes, to frame me."

"And why would he want to do that?" The young man sounded tired.

"Because he's got some sort of shady operation going on in the hotel and he doesn't want me to find out more about it and stop him. He slashed my tyres to warn me."

"The hotel manager slashed your tyres? Did you report that?"

"Not to the police no." Stupid idiot that I am. "But I made a report for the hotel bosses."

"Did you see him do it?"

"No."

"Are there any witnesses who saw him do it?"

"No." Isn't it odd how the truth can sound so bizarre? I sounded hysterical even to myself, so I made a big effort to calm myself down. "I've got a receipt for four new tyres. The mechanic will tell you they were slashed."

"But not who slashed them – unless he was there." He was irritatingly logical.

"Look, I just think you should consider the possibility that there was more than one key that could open my locker." I replied as quietly and calmly as I could. I wanted to scream at him, 'How dare you doubt my integrity even for one moment? Don't you realise that I'm a truthful person and Poliakov is a devious, manipulating bully who's up to no good?' But he was just a boy doing his job. This was another mundane case requiring lots of paperwork and bringing no glory. A post-menopausal woman indulging in a bit of petty theft – yawn. Bring on a good, gory murder investigation. Well if I got my hands on Poliakov, he might have a murder to investigate, yet!

Sometimes I have little premonitions. Whenever I had attempted to imagine myself in my new role on my first morning in the office, I couldn't squeeze myself into the picture however hard I tried. Me and Poliakov, sitting at adjacent desks – it was never going to happen, I'd been convinced of that. But I'd had no idea that an accusation of theft would be the obstacle. I had thought the tyres had been my 'warning' to behave myself and not to accept the promotion, maybe even to leave the hotel. But I hadn't taken the warning and Poliakov had proved more determined and more devious than I had imagined. He'd managed effectively to exclude me, not just from the office but also from the hotel. I was suspended from work, pending the investigation, and even if I weren't prosecuted – the evidence was entirely circumstantial – the hotel certainly wouldn't take me back. Worse even than that, he had made me unemployable. Who would hire a chambermaid who'd been interviewed by the police for theft? Who would employ me at all? I'd never get another job. How would I manage? The only saving grace was that my mother wasn't alive to see this day.

"Come on, we need a drink," Sheila dragged me out of my miserable conjecture as we hit the street.

"Shall we go to Ma Preston's?"

"Bugger Ma Preston's, we both need something more fortifying than tea," and she marched me to the nearest pub. At just after eleven, we were the only customers and were served instantly.

"Don't say anything until you've drunk that," Sheila said, placing a large glass of brandy on the table in front of me. "I've ordered coffee to follow. We need some brain resuscitation before we see the solicitor."

"I wish you hadn't made the appointment," I said. The brandy began instantly to relax and unknot a little the tangle in the pit of my stomach that had been there ever since that first shock of seeing the purse in my locker.

"Having representation will show them that you won't let yourself be pushed around."

"But I can't afford it, I told you."

"And I told you it's an early Christmas present from me. Why are you such a stubborn bitch, Prudence Baxter? You need help. Just shut up and accept it." You can always rely on Sheila to be subtle. "It's Marc Clark we need on our side," she continued. "Bloody awful timing his being in the States."

"Perfect timing for Ivan, don't you see? While the cat's away… "

"Well I told Phil to try and get hold of him."

"But of course, Phil has his number," I brightened.

"Has he?"

"Well yes of course," I tried to find a reason for my certainty other than the real one that Phil and Mr Clark were dressing-up buddies. "I mean they're old school friends, aren't they?"

"School was a long time ago." Sheila clearly thought I was clutching at straws. "But we'll get hold of him somehow. I'm sure he'll clear the whole thing up at once."

I couldn't confess to Sheila that I was less confident of Mr C's help. I had given the man reasons out of my own mouth to doubt my integrity. After all if I could contemplate selling his story to the *Daily Mail*, why would I not snatch a purse from a guest? If he refused to believe I was innocent, I would only have myself to blame. But if he didn't believe me, what hope was there? I downed the remains of my brandy feeling its warmth dissolving the last of those knots and heating my blood.

"Ivan," I said, slapping the table and making Sheila almost take a bite out of her glass. "I can't just rely on Mr C to rescue me, I have to get Poliakov myself. I've got nothing else to do all day – thanks to him. I'm going to haunt that Siberian vampire and find out just what he's up to and then give all the evidence to Mr C. Ivan may be terrible, but he's going to wish he'd never crossed swords with Prudence Baxter."

"Or Sheila Riley." Sheila clinked her empty glass against mine and to seal our pact, we upended them letting the very last drops of brandy drain down our throats.

# Chapter Thirty

Three days after the day of shame at the police station, there was a meeting at Sheila's to report on the progress of the investigations that Sheila and I had named 'Operation GIN - Get Ivan Nailed.' We had roped Moira and Matthew into the campaign so they also came along and the meeting was in danger of turning into a social evening. Sheila had made a delicious goulash and Phil kept topping up glasses, which made it difficult to call the meeting to order. Finally they asked me to set the ball rolling, by telling them what I'd discovered from my observation of the Bijou. I had a full report, which I began to read.

"06.30 hours: took up my surveillance position outside the service entrance of the Bijou Hotel. A bit nippy. Definitely need the tights on under the trousers. Fairly hard to look as if I'm casually loitering in this temperature and at this hour of the morning. Hope no one calls the police.

06.45: Mrs A passes by and stops to chat. There's a new woman doing my shift - a hefty blonde who speaks no English. When Mrs A talks to her she just points to her impressive chest and says 'alona' which might be her name or her status. Mrs A agrees to lurk in service room until the laundry lorry arrives. I stay here, we thus create a pincer movement.

06.58: laundry lorry hurtles round corner. I glance quickly down and pretend to be looking at a message on my phone. My disguise – curly wig belonging to RATS – slips forward. It's too big. Don't think the guys in the lorry notice. Beefy young man hangs out of driver's side door and presses numbers on a keypad by the gate.

06.59: service gates begin to open and lorry passes into courtyard of Bijou Hotel. Gates start to close automatically. Realise I'll see bugger-all from here, so fling myself through the gap before gates shut and dodge behind organic waste bin."

"Pru," Matthew interrupted my recital. "Fascinating style you have, quite unique. Love the immediacy, but it might be more constructive just to summarise the pertinent points for us."

"Tell us what you found out and cut the crap," Sheila translated.

I protested that I had half an A4 notepad. I had thought it of the utmost importance to keep a precise log and I wasn't at all sure that I could make a précis, just like that.

"Did you see anything suspicious?" Moira asked. "I can tell you that the laundry company is legitimate. I went over to Earl Shilton to check them out. They are an Asian family-run business operating over the East Midlands."

"Well, what they do isn't legit. I saw them," I answered. "It's just as I thought. They go in and out in the laundry skip. I could never work out why we needed Savoy Hotel-size skips for the Bijou laundry. It didn't make sense, but now it does."

"Who goes in and out, Pru?" Phil wanted to know. He always demands precision.

"People, well, two men at least – inside the laundry skip.

They've got this forklift contraption to lift the skips in and out of the lorry. I thought that was odd. They're strapping lads, the driver and his mate: they could easily lift the skip between them. I thought it was 'Health and Safety' but now I know it's because they've got people inside the skip."

"But I still don't understand who you saw," Phil persisted.

"People who shouldn't be there. People who they want to hide. I don't know who they are and I don't think I should speculate like some BBC News reporter, I'm just reporting what I saw."

"People trafficking," Matthew said, scenting a crime and human-interest story for his magazine programme, and stealing my punchline.

"Did you get any pictures?" Sheila asked. This was embarrassing. I had had my phone with me ready to take photos, but their heads appeared over the top of the skip for such a short time, and I'd had to move so quickly, that I'd held the phone the wrong way round.

"You took a selfie in that wig?" cackled Sheila. "Let's have a look."

"Later," said Headmaster Phil. "We have to stick to the evidence."

"Transporting people in the laundry," said Matt, "with or without the knowledge of the laundry company. This could be a big story."

"Pity you didn't get that photo, Pru," Phil sighed.

"I did take pictures of all the people who went into or came out of the hotel during the day – obviously through the front door." I wanted to exonerate my previous mistake. "Nothing suspicious there though. They were mostly Yorkists."

"Well, I've done some research on the victim of the theft, our Ms Liashenko," Matthew was twinkling, falling over himself to produce 'exhibit A' for the defence.

"I haven't finished my evidence yet," I protested. I perused my notes, making him and everyone else wait. "I followed Poliakov when he left the hotel at 18.53. He didn't do anything suspicious – apart from being attached to his mobile the whole way from the Bijou to his flat in Highfields." I waited again while they registered the significance of the place name – an area of high Victoriana with a very low reputation. "I felt a bit uncomfortable watching his flat, so I didn't hang around. I mean a couple of cars slowed right down… "

"You were very fetching in that wig," laughed Sheila.

"So, I didn't stay long. There was a man sitting in a car parked just down the road from Ivan's flat. He was pretending to read a newspaper, but he couldn't possibly have seen in that light."

"But to come back to Ms Liashenko," Matthew tried again.

"I was getting to her," I protested. "I have got a photo of her." I found the picture on my phone and passed it round. "Standing on a street corner, two streets away from Poliakov's flat."

"She's not doing a traffic census, is she?" Sheila remarked, and passed the phone on.

"Are you sure it's the same woman?" asked Moira. "I hope you don't let women like that into the hotel as paying guests?"

"It's her all right. I'm not likely to forget that face. But she was more substantially covered the last time I saw her."

"As I have been trying to tell you," Matthew persevered,

"Elena Liashenko was a Ukrainian figure skater. Competed in the European Championships and the Olympics. Whilst it's quite possible that our Ms Liashenko's parents named her after a local heroine, I think it more likely that she gave a false name to the police."

"And a false address," added Moira. "I went to the address Sheila found in the hotel registration, and guess what?"

"It doesn't exist. You've rather given that away, cherub," said Matthew.

"It does exist, Mr Know-it-all. Number 57a Grace Dieu Road does exist. There's a dog-grooming parlour on the ground floor and a chiropodist above, but no living accommodation. I went into both places and asked for Elena or Ms Liashenko and no one had heard of her."

"Let's summarise what we have so far," Phil began taking charge again. "We've discredited Liashenko, or whoever she is, but we still don't have proof that her purse didn't get stolen at the Bijou, or that Pru didn't take it."

"We need to be able to connect her definitively with Poliakov," Matthew added.

"She was plying her trade very close to his flat," said Sheila.

"We know people are being smuggled out of the hotel in the laundry skip," I reminded them of my discovery.

"But we have nothing to connect them with Poliakov," Phil reminded me.

"There's his card left on my trolley and the fact that he's always lurking in the service room," I said.

"Was he lurking there yesterday morning?" Sheila asked.

"Mrs A didn't see him, no."

"Bugger!"

"But did she see the men in the skip?" Phil asked.

"No, they must have got in there before she arrived."

"All the info is in that back office," said Sheila. "No wonder he didn't want Pru in there. I did try to convince him, when I was playing the UK Tourist Board official, to show me the computer systems. I told him that we at the East Midlands Tourist Enhancement Board could supply him with free hotel management software. But he was having none of it. Just kept saying 'privacy' like a demented parrot."

"Privacy, yes and we know whose," I said.

"I did manage to have a word with Doleful Dave," Sheila continued. "Frightened the life out of him at first when I crept into the boiler room. I think he thought I was a time and motion expert." She laughed. Only I got that joke. "He's got some scheme hatched to trick Ivan into making a duplicate locker key. But I think Poliakov's too astute to fall for that one."

"We need a proper investigation of this Poliakov," Matthew said. "I've begun putting word out about him, but it's delicate work. On the surface he's a model citizen. He's been at his present address since the Bijou opened, pays his bills regularly… "

"Goes to church three times on Sundays," Sheila mocked.

"And pockets the collection, plate and all," I said.

"What about Marc's business partner, the man who appointed him?" Phil asked, pleased to have suggested a new lead. "Anything there?"

"Gavin Strutt," said Matthew. "I've only got access to the 'for-public-consumption' type stuff so far. Local man, self-made in scrap metal."

"Must weigh a ton," Sheila interrupted and she and Moira laughed.

"He has lots of business interests," Matthew continued unperturbed, "including nightclubs and at least one other hotel. Quite a few overseas interests, nothing yet though to connect him with Russia or the Ukraine. But I've got contacts doing some digging for me." Matt was enjoying the importance 'contacts' doing his bidding lent him. Phil drew the meeting to a close.

"I'll open another bottle," he said. "Let's drink to teamwork." He went into the kitchen and returned with another red and a corkscrew. "By the way, the team's about to get bigger. I've spoken to Marc and he'll be back on Tuesday. Says he'll drive straight up from Heathrow. Seems to think you're a VIP, Pru." The others laughed, missing the smile Phil gave me and its significance. Only I understood the significance of that.

# Chapter Thirty-one

It's the first today. I should be starting my new job, snuggling up with Ivan in the back office. Instead I'm trailing him around town. I must admit I prefer keeping my distance from him, though I do wish I hadn't lost my job. I've kept up the surveillance but I've abandoned the RATS wig and instead I'm wearing a pair of dark-framed glasses and quite a thick pull-on hat. It's making my head sweat.

15.34: Subject has left bank where he spent some time at the statement and transfers machines and is now heading towards the Clock Tower, glued as usual to his phone. He has quite a leisurely walk. Swings his right hip further forward than his left, which gives his body a slight twist. I never noticed that before. He hunches his left shoulder too. Must have had a serious accident at some time.

15.38: Subject enters shopping mall. Don't suppose he'll be stopping for a chocolate-chip cookie though, let alone buying me one. Could do with a cup of tea.

15.44: He's not shopping. Doesn't even look at the windows. Exits mall and enters staircase to car park. Very odd. He doesn't have a car. Perhaps he's going to steal coins from the parking machines.

15.46: Up to third floor. Thought I'd lost him. I had to let him turn the corner of the stairwell before I followed.

He's in the far corner as I cross the exit lane, pretending to look for my car. He's talking to two young men. Both taller than him – though that's not difficult – both wearing jeans, leather jackets and beanie hats. They turn to look in my direction. Oh my God! I bob down behind a Smart car wishing it were a Range Rover, and do a little pantomime of having dropped my key. When I dare look out again – no one. Bugger, I can't have lost them. No car has pulled out. Go along row of parked cars to check. Just a mum with shopping, pushchair and whingeing toddler, approaching car. Conclude suspect must have gone back to stairwell.

15.50 (Or around then.): Go back to stairwell. No one on the stairs going up or down. Listen intently but no footsteps ascending or descending. Decide to try 'up' staircase first. Arrive at first landing and prepare to turn. Something blocks the light. Two people coming down, fast. Two men, in jeans, leather jackets and beanie hats. They're going to collide with me. They haven't seen me. Yes they have. I just see the eyes of one of them. They are Alwin's violet-blue eyes and they're laughing at me. I'm unbalanced, lifted off my feet; I make a grab. There must be something solid to hold me back, but there's nothing, just smooth, painted walls. I realise I'm falling. I'm heading backwards down the stairs towards the landing. I seem to have a lot of time for my brain to talk to me, 'This can only end badly,' it says. The ground finally rises up to smack me and I realise I am not on my feet. I can see my left hand because I'm lying on my left side. I'm scrunched up. I can hear things too – footsteps hurtling down stairs. Fire doors slamming.

A man appears out of nowhere to help me. He tells me to lie still. Why would he think I'm in any rush to move?

If I move I'll know what I've broken because it will hurt. It can't be my neck at least, because I can feel my toes. I know where they are even though I can't see them and when I tell the fingers of my left hand to move, they open and close. Gingerly I try moving each limb in turn. Fortunately they all make a slow response. There's no sharp pain as I risk a stretch, so maybe nothing's broken after all. I fell like a rag doll. I did whack my head, but the hat cushioned me a little. I'll probably have whiplash tomorrow and be black and blue. I try to sit up and find I'm trembling all over. The man is very kind, talking to me all the time. He's already called an ambulance, despite my protests that there's no need, really. It's true that, as I pull myself to my knees and then stagger to my feet with his help, my knees and ankles buckle, but I know it's shock and fear not physical damage causing me to crumple. He doesn't ask me what happened.

I thanked the man but I didn't get his name. I lost sight of him in the little crowd of ghouls who stopped to stare as I was loaded into the ambulance and whisked away, at great speed with sirens blaring, to a two-hour wait in A & E. There was nothing broken, and I didn't have concussion – not even a headache – just a sore bump where head hit concrete. I thought of all those people in my life who'd told me I was hard-headed. Wouldn't they love to know they were right? My left ankle is a bit stiff. They strapped it up and dabbed at the abrasions that had appeared on all the bits of me that stuck out as I had landed. They asked me what had happened and I told them I had been knocked into by some careless people and fallen down a flight of stairs. All the time I was telling them I could see they didn't believe me. I was too scared just to have been the victim of an accident. But I didn't want to say out loud 'I was attacked and pushed down the stairs by thugs, on the orders of my ex-boss who's an even bigger thug', not because I wanted to hide it from them, but because I couldn't deal with that reality.

I called a taxi to go home and didn't consider the expense. I didn't call Sheila or Moira because I couldn't face being fussed over. Once I got home I ran myself a bath and sank into it with a glass of sherry. The warmth of the water and the alcohol took quick effect. My muscles began to relax and the trembling and chattering of teeth gradually subsided. I tried to focus my mind on pleasant aspects of life: snowdrops, milk chocolate digestives – anything except what had just happened.

I was in my dressing gown, towel round my head, about to call Sheila, when my doorbell rang. It seemed to me very late – too late for visitors – but a glance at the kitchen clock showed me it was only just after eight. I found I couldn't move to answer the door. I was suddenly afraid. No one just came to visit, they always phoned first. No elections in the offing so no canvassers, no one selling things at this time of day; charity collection? They could call again. Might Sheila have heard about my fall and come to check up on me? The doorbell rang again. Whoever it was wasn't going away, and I couldn't cower in the kitchen for the rest of the night, so I picked up a fearsome kitchen knife and went to the door shouting:

"Who is it?"

"It's Marc Clark, Miss Baxter. I hope I'm not disturbing you." I opened the door.

"How are you, Miss Baxter?" I was too stunned to do anything normal like invite him in. I just stood there in my dressing gown with towel turban, clutching the knife – a novel reworking of *Psycho*. "To misquote Mae West," he said, "are you glad to see me or is that a weapon in your hand?" It took me a moment to react and lower the knife.

"Sorry, come in. Do come in." He thrust a cellophane-wrapped bunch of flowers at me and took advantage of my confusion to place them in my right hand, in exchange for the knife. "Thank you," I managed, and looked at the flowers: white lilies and pink gerberas. Therapeutic colours, hedging his bets – white in case I was already dead and pink for the convalescent.

"Is it convenient to talk for a moment?" he asked, reminding me that we were still standing in the hall with the front door open. I showed him into the kitchen – the only warm room. He refused sherry but said he'd kill for a cup of real English tea. I shuffled towards the kettle to fill it.

"Now you just sit down," he said. "Let me get the tea. I'm sure I can find all the necessaries." I did as I was told and sank onto a chair. For the first time since the incident I felt the urge to cry. I wanted to thank him, but when I tried to say, 'What lovely flowers,' I found my voice was completely unreliable – better to keep quiet. He took the flowers from me, filled a glass of water and stuck the stems into it. I watched all his actions as if I'd been robbed of movement.

"What did the doctors say?" he asked.

"How do you know about… ?" My voice was still not completely cooperating.

"It was one of our research team who put you into the ambulance. I gave him a hard time for not going with you."

"Oh no, you ought not to have. He was very kind, very

kind indeed. It was fortunate he was there." I was missing something. "How did he happen to be there?"

"I put someone onto watching the hotel before I left for the States." He sat down at the table opposite me. "What you told me – the rooms disturbed and all – didn't make sense to me, but I always follow things up, and in any case I already had my doubts about Poliakov."

"Ivan, we called him – the Terrible." I shivered. "You know he had my tyres slashed?"

"Yes, that was his first mistake. You must really have rattled him. Well, thanks to his own mistakes he's on his way to being exposed and deposed." He jumped up to make the tea as the kettle switched itself off. He began to fill the teapot. "But you still haven't told me how you are. You're not in plaster, but what did the doctors say?"

"I'm fine, just a bit bruised. I'll be stiff tomorrow." I experimented, stretching out my left elbow, which had taken a direct hit. It didn't respond well. "I'm glad I won't have to go on surveillance tomorrow if you've got your man watching him."

"No," he put the teapot on the table and covered it with the cosy. "I'm sorry you got involved in this at all. It's not pleasant. Stay away from the hotel and leave things to the professionals. It's important that you take care of yourself. The hotel will pick up any bills you have for physiotherapy and such." The same urge to cry almost overwhelmed me. "And don't worry about your job," he continued. "I know you didn't take that purse. Gut instinct," he said, smiled and patted his waist. I forced a very weak smile in response. He got up and began opening cupboards. "Got any biscuits?"

"In the larder," I pointed to the door, careful to use my right arm.

"You have a larder," he laughed. "How delightfully quaint. We had a larder in the prefab. I thought they died out with the invention of fridge-freezers." He returned to the table with some hobnobs. "This is quite some house. I'll bet you can give fabulous parties here."

"There've been none in living memory. You can't see it in the dark but the whole thing is falling down."

"I hope we have time to finish our tea before we evacuate" he said, pouring the tea and handing me a mug.

"How was your trip?" A bit late to be the polite hostess I realised.

"Excellent. The First World War documentary is a 'done deal', thanks to Natalie's preparations. They are also very keen on my fronting a series on unsolved crimes in history. They like a British accent. Makes what's being said more authoritative and trustworthy. Natalie's already got someone working on the scripts."

"That sounds very exciting," I said. Wouldn't mind a job like that myself, I didn't say. "So you'll be moving to America soon?" He put down his mug suddenly.

"This is Cape Kennedy house, isn't it? That's amazing."

"It's called The Tower, but I never use the name. The postman… "

"Every other Sunday," he explained, "we used to go on the bus to visit my Gran. She lived in one of the almshouses in Knighton. And we'd pass this house with a rocket attached to it – like a launch pad with the moon rockets. You could just see it from the top deck of the bus." He stretched his legs out under the table. "I can't believe I'm sitting in it drinking tea and eating hobnobs. You'd better take them away from me." He pushed the packet towards me. "I used to tell my mum that one day I'd buy the house and we'd launch the rocket." That made me laugh even though my ribs objected.

"Make me an offer and it's yours."

"I wonder," he looked across to the door. "I mean when you've finished your tea – only maybe you're too tired. No, it's all right. Maybe another time."

Of course I had to show him round the house after that. I apologised as we wandered from one cold, damp room to another and winced to see the house as he must have been seeing it – a great disappointment with nothing the way he'd imagined it. But if it was all a let-down, he didn't tell me.

"I always imagined you'd wear spacesuits in the house – everyone sitting around the dining table with goldfish bowls on their heads," he confessed.

"A hard hat would probably be a better idea these days," I said. "This is the tower room, your rocket. There isn't much to see and I'm afraid we can't go upstairs. The floor is rotten."

"Can't it be saved?"

"Yes, for an emperor's ransom," I sighed, "which I don't have."

"That's such a pity." He stood looking up at the stains on the ceiling and the damp around the cornice, then looked at me. "I'm sorry. You must be really tired. I shouldn't keep you on your feet talking like this. I only came to see how you were." He began heading towards the hallway and the front door. "Will you be all right on your own, or do you want me to call someone?"

"I'll be fine," I said, and caught sight of myself in the hall mirror. I saw what he was seeing: strained face almost as white as my forgotten headgear, big, panda eyes and not just from where the mascara had run. I suddenly felt like Methuselah's much older sister. He caught me staring at myself.

"What you need is a good night's sleep," he advised.

"I'll be fine," I repeated. He still wasn't convinced. Out of an inside pocket he produced a business card.

"My number. Call me for anything."

"Thank you. You're very kind," I just managed to say and opened the door. He turned on the doorstep.

"The hotel will be needing a new manager once we've dealt with Poliakov, but we can talk about that another time. Sleep well." I closed the door after him and when I was sure he'd gone, leant against it and finally gave in to the urge to have a really good cry.

# Chapter Thirty-two

As it happens I didn't need Mr Clark's injunction to keep me away from the hotel surveillance this morning, for when I woke up I made an instant and important discovery. I found I had more muscles than I had ever thought possible, some in places I hadn't visited for years, and every one of them was saying, 'Get off my case!' In fact I hurt so much I wondered if the staff in A & E hadn't overlooked a few hairline fractures. You hear such stories about the NHS. But in any case just sitting up was like prising open hinges rusted over centuries. Leaving the house, even leaving my bed, was beyond my strength.

Sheila, alerted to the situation by my phone call yesterday evening, had come straight over to see me. When she hadn't been able to carry me off back to her house, she had taken instead a front door key so that she could check in on me this morning without disturbing me. That way I got a cup of tea without having to drag my rigid frame into the kitchen. In fact, when she saw how incapacitated I was, she brought me in breakfast, as well as a thermos of hot soup for lunch, and I burst into tears. I keep having little weepy sessions, most unlike me. I hope it's a temporary thing as it's deeply embarrassing and crying really hurts the ribs on my left side. What's worse, this morning's crying fit meant that I had to send Sheila for the box of tissues in the bathroom knowing full well that I hadn't cleaned in there for over a week. She left the house around nine and press-ganged Moira into joining her at the hotel for joint surveillance duties. That way the two of them discovered some of the day's proceedings at the Bijou and brought me home the story. Mr Clark's phone call in the evening filled me in on the rest.

When they arrived at the hotel just before ten, everything seemed normal. Poliakov was nowhere in sight, which was perfectly normal. Moira needed an excuse to hang around the foyer area and so she began a linguistic tussle with the receptionist, asking her about the possibility of organising a wedding anniversary celebration, a buffet for fifty guests, at some imagined date in the future. According to Sheila, Moira is a very convincing fantasist and had even begun to sketch table settings on the message pad. However the manager was 'unavailable' and a tour of the facilities at that time was 'not possible', so Moira asked if she could be served coffee in the foyer whilst she waited for the manager to become 'available'.

Sheila, meanwhile, had taken the backdoor approach and gone in search of Dave or Mrs A. She found Dave first in his usual hiding place, but unusually he was very animated. There had been a real panic this morning at the service entrance. When the laundry van had arrived and the driver had keyed in the usual entry code, the gate had remained resolutely shut. Dave had just set foot inside the hotel when Poliakov had yelled at him to 'come quick'. The code, overnight, had decided not to work. Dave had had to disconnect the whole system before the gate could be opened manually. That delay had cost the delivery van driver a good forty minutes, but he had waited, all the time swearing his head off at Poliakov. Dave said:

"Even ice-man Ivan was sweating."

"Why had the code changed? Was it a problem with the system?" Sheila asked.

"Could be. But my bet is someone changed it."

"Poliakov?"

"Not 'im. Unless he's a damned good actor, he knew note about it. 'e looked frit to me and that van driver was mega-agitated. 'e was ready to land one on Mr P.," Dave chuckled. "Now that would have bin wuth seeing."

"Who do you think changed the code then, and why?" asked Sheila.

"Search me, but there's summat else not right. Guess who was hanging round with Ivan?" Of course Sheila had no idea and Dave was bursting to tell her anyway. "Young Alwin – him what worked here as a bellboy, then got the push for being light-fingered. I thought, what's he doing here when he's bin sacked? Chucking himself at the gate he was, trying to make it open – daft bugger. You'd need a tank to move that. Ivan sent him off sharpish when I got there. He sacked him for thievin' then has him hanging about the hotel. Makes no sense to me that."

Sheila also hung around and caught Mrs A as she was returning her trolley. She'd had a bad start to her morning too. Poliakov hadn't let her into the cleaning store to get her equipment. There had been voices in the room, even shouting, but she had seen no one because Poliakov had wheeled out her trolley and shoved it at her and sent her away without letting her check her supplies. She was going to be late now for her lady in Glenfield.

Moira then took over the story and explained that after a long wait she had tackled the receptionist again and asked her to find Poliakov. She had begun to feel irritated, as if she really had got a party to organise. In mid-conversation, she had seen Mr Clark crossing the floor towards them. With him were two men, one of them a uniformed police officer.

"Do excuse me, Madam," Mr Clark interrupted her non-conversation with the receptionist and addressed the startled-looking girl. "These gentlemen need to speak to Mr Poliakov on a pressing matter. Will you please call him for me?" The receptionist didn't seem able to speak so Moira said:

"I've been waiting to see him for over an hour. He doesn't seem to be available." She watched as the group made their way into the back office, but returned empty-handed. Mr Clark took out his phone and selected a number. He waited a few moments then said to his companions:

"Number unavailable. I'll see where my team are." He selected another number. As he was waiting, two more men appeared at the entrance to the hotel escorting a third – a young man in jeans and a leather jacket. He was brought to the reception desk and then both groups crowded into the back office. Mr Clark turned to Moira to apologise:

"I'm very sorry, Madam, that the manager isn't here to help. Perhaps the receptionist can assist you." Moira said the girl was beyond speech and she offered to go and get her a coffee, but she didn't seem to be taking anything in either. She just watched alongside Moira as the young man was escorted to the police van waiting outside the entrance.

I got the last pieces of the puzzle when Mr Clark phoned me:

"My investigators kept an eye on the empty suites over the course of several nights and saw groups of up to four men and another of three women being shepherded into them," Mr Clark explained.

"Shepherded by whom, Poliakov?"

"No, he was never there. It was a couple of young men. The ones who pushed you down the stairs. That's why we had to leave everything as it was until we could connect Poliakov with the operation. My people set up a hidden camera in the cleaning store and blocked the van this morning with the changed entry code. We got video footage of Poliakov pushing some of the poor devils into the laundry skip and out onto the van. He was in such a hurry this morning he didn't check the room for surveillance."

"And were they immigrants, as I thought?"

"Yes, all Eastern Europeans. The police intercepted the van this morning and also picked up the ones left behind at the hotel. I think we've wrapped the whole thing up."

"The poor souls."

"Yes, but at least the slavery bit's all over for them."

"Terrible," was all I could add. It was hard to believe I'd complained about my job as chambermaid when all the time I'd been in the midst of real misery and exploitation.

"Anyway, how are you?" he asked.

"Oh, you know. A bit creaky, but it's beginning to wear off. I'm certainly better for knowing that Poliakov and young Alwin won't be standing on my street corner." The line went quiet and I was afraid we'd been cut off. Then he said:

"They still have to pick up Poliakov. I'm afraid our little trick this morning with the gates gave him a warning. The police are hoping he'll lead them to the boss."

"They have him under surveillance?"

"Not exactly, no. But don't worry, he won't show up here again. My guess is that he's already left the country."

"But they can't let him escape. That's not fair."

"Nobody wants to catch him more than me – unless it's Gavin. He appointed him."

"Pity you didn't appoint me manager and save yourselves all this trouble."

"We intend to do just that, Pru, once you're fit enough to return to work."

# Chapter Thirty-three

One of my first tasks as the new temporary acting manager of the Bijou Hotel was to organise the press conference called by Mr Clark. Phil couldn't get time off work, but the rest of the Operation GIN team, Sheila, Moira and Matthew, came along arriving twenty minutes before the scheduled start. I'd had the large meeting room prepared. Facing the rows of chairs we had put a table with two more chairs behind it, for Mr Clark and the detective. Dave had set up microphones and was there, trailing cable and endeavouring to stick it safely to the carpet. Having already cleaned the room, and brought in supplies of water and glasses, Mrs A was seated at the back near the window.

"Miss Pru, Miss Sheila, come and sit wi' me." I went over and introduced her to Moira and Matt. "Now you manager you too proud to sit wi' the cleanin' lady, hey?" She chuckled merrily and squeezed my arm.

"Temporary acting manager," I corrected her. Marc had hinted that I could set my sights higher, but I didn't tell her that.

"This could all have turned out very differently," he had said when asking me to set up the press conference. "Imagine the egg on my face if some local hack had discovered my hotel was being used as a staging post by a group of people traffickers." As his own team had uncovered the operation he was able to take the spotlight and face the press confidently, as the scourge of wrongdoers and the discoverer of the truth, his reputation, and that of the hotel, intact.

"Save me a place," I said. "I just need to do another quick check to see that everything's all right, then I'll join you."

In the front rows were TV cameramen and reporters from the local channels. Matt fell over himself to go and greet them and come back to us with their names.

"And who's that balding chap with the scrunched-up ears?" Moira wanted to know. "He seems familiar." Matt was defeated. Forced to admit that he didn't know him he said:

"There are journalists from the national press too. Got wind of a good crime-busting story involving illegal immigrants and a TV celeb, and scuttled up the M1."

As Marc came into the room, I saw that he had with him the same young detective who had been compelled to sit through the boredom of my interview. The translation of Poliakov's statement, when they caught him, would be worth his while reading.

"Ladies and gentlemen," Marc began as soon as everyone was settled. "The twenty-first century is only just over a decade old, but it continues to throw up surprises. Most of us believe that slavery is dead. We know from our history that the Slave Trade – that shameful stain on the past of our country – ended in 1833. It therefore beggars belief that another kind of slave trade is still being carried on right now, across the country, in our towns, right under our noses. Through the vigilance of key members of my hotel staff, whom I cannot thank enough–"

A 'Well said' from Sheila interrupted him. Matt flapped at her and Sheila mockingly flapped back at him.

"...and the expertise of the team from my programme, *The Truth*, we have uncovered a group engaged in the despicable trafficking of illegal immigrants, using this hotel and several other innocent local firms, as its base.

For me, traffickers are the lowest forms of life. They take advantage of the natural human desire to seek a better life, and turn those they catch in their trap into bonded labourers, who will never be free of their debts. I am personally outraged that they had the nerve to try to practise their evil trade in my newly opened hotel. But ultimately, I am relieved that once again the truth has prevailed, and that the justice system will soon put those remorseless traffickers behind bars where they belong." Enthusiastic clapping from Sheila and Mrs A, who urged us to join in. Matthew slid down in his seat as reporters turned to stare.

"I will hand you over to Detective Sergeant Cresswell, who will give you a precise breakdown of the investigation, and then we will take your questions."

I already knew the story that the young policeman began to tell the journalists, but I still found it hard to credit that Poliakov's group, just one in a chain according to the evidence gathered, had got away with it for so long. It was also odd that Marc hadn't mentioned his business partner , Gavin Strutt, or the fact that it was he who had appointed Poliakov in the first place. True, Ivan didn't have a criminal record – at least not one that had bobbed to the surface so far – but neither could he be said to be above board. For example he didn't appear to satisfy any of the criteria for the right of residence in the UK. Almost anyone would have been a better manager and

I'm sure a few locals would have been equally well-qualified for the job of chief slave master, had the position ever been advertised. How he entered the country and how he got the job at the Bijou were still unanswered questions.

Moira drew my attention to the Asian family, owners of the Spick and Span Laundry Co. They were listening intently to Sgt Cresswell's description of how two of their employees had made a little extra for themselves, in company time, by acting as a courier service for their human packages. Diverting from their schedule a little, they had called at the warehouse where the immigrants – mostly nationals of states formally part of the USSR – had been dumped. They then reverted to their daily rounds and drove their passengers to the Bijou Hotel and other locations within the city limits. There, in their ones and twos, the immigrants could more easily be integrated into the workforce, find a safe house, or in the Bijou's case an empty suite, to hole up in, before being made to disappear again when and wherever another enterprise called for dirt-cheap labour.

Poliakov, whose own entry date into the UK remained a bit of a mystery, got a percentage of the fee paid by the immigrants for their 'work permit', got a fee from the employers who used these unfortunates, and in the case of the Bijou's employees, pocketed their whole 'salary'. Sgt Cresswell didn't believe Poliakov to have been the 'big boss'. As yet they still had no further leads on Poliakov or his boss and had to appeal for anyone knowing Poliakov's whereabouts to come forward with information.

In their questions the journalists seemed to be most interested in figures. How many immigrants had been smuggled? How much money had the traffickers made? How much had the immigrants each paid for their passage into slavery?

"None of your media friends seems very interested in the outcome for those poor immigrants," lamented Moira.

"That's because they already know the outcome," said Matt. "If they are caught, like the two working here, they will be deported. If not, they'll just continue in servitude – unless they manage to escape."

"But it seems so unfair. Surely one of your colleagues could champion them. I mean they've lost all that money. They'll have nothing when they get back."

"What do you suggest we do – pass round the hat?" Matt sneered.

"Your lady is right," Mrs A agreed. "Ivan take their money and give them nothin'. And when they catch him and lock him up in his nice prison cell with colour TV, who pay? You and me is who."

"What I want to know," said Sheila, "… in fact I'm going to ask." She stood up before Matt could stop her. Unaware of the fact that she was an invited guest, not a member of the press, Sgt Cresswell signalled that he would take her question.

"My question is really for Mr Clark," she said. "How the hell did you come to appoint a shit like Poliakov as manager in the first place?" Matt was beside himself, and even I felt rather embarrassed by the bluntness of her question, and the pressure she was putting on Marc in front of the media. He didn't falter though.

"A good question, and a little plain Anglo-Saxon always spices things up. I take full responsibility for the decision and its consequences, but I'm afraid I have to fall back on the old excuse that I didn't do it. The decision to appoint him was made by my business partner and co-owner of the hotel, Gavin Strutt, who unfortunately has another engagement and isn't able to be here today to explain himself to you."

"Is Gavin Strutt involved with the traffickers?" Sheila persisted.

"I think Sgt Cresswell should answer that one," Marc replied.

"Mr Strutt does not figure in our investigations," Sgt Cresswell confirmed.

"Then perhaps he should," Sheila advised.

Another journalist then asked Marc if he regretted having opened the hotel in view of all the problems he'd had.

"I always think regrets are pointless," Marc said. "I am very sorry that my debut in the world of hotels and leisure has had this setback. I'm deeply sorry it has been the cause of suffering to anyone. It's a terrible situation for the immigrants, and it has also been dangerous for members of my staff who were harassed and physically attacked on the orders of Poliakov. No employee should have to face danger simply as a result of doing his or her job well. But, that said, I am very proud indeed of my hotel and, Poliakov excepted, the excellent group of people I have who run it. Let's not forget they are the ones who quickly suspected Poliakov and alerted me. I am confident I can leave the hotel in their capable hands and go on with my plans to make a series of history documentaries."

"This is an unbelievably good piece of publicity for your programme, *The Truth*. Is it just coincidence?" one journalist asked, making people laugh. "Will it be in the new series when it starts?"

"That's the producer's decision," said Marc. "And you all know how unpredictable producers are." Matt forced a laugh. "But, at least I can promise her the inside story on this one."

# Chapter Thirty-four

I needed to appoint some new staff since the receptionists had been arrested and Lev, the bellboy, had disappeared into the ether at the first sight of blue uniforms approaching the hotel. I've taken on Sharifa and Joanna as receptionists – both speak English – and a nice young lad called Shane, as bellboy. After all I couldn't hold him to account for his name. He looks very smart in his uniform, gives a perfect first impression of the hotel because the jacket collar almost covers his tattoo. He's got a cobra coiled round his neck and goodness knows what else on other surfaces. You can still just see the hood of the cobra bobbing up towards his left ear as he's walking around. It bothered me but I seem to be in a tiny minority of those repelled by painted flesh. But as I discovered when I conducted the interviews, today's youths don't come in unilluminated versions. He's very enthusiastic and just the sort of smiley face you want to see in a hotel lobby. He's efficient too and soon had glasses unpacked and drinks and canapés set up in the Valkyrie Suite, ready for the intimate cocktails Marc wanted to offer to the staff to thank us all once again.

It was odd to be back in the Valkyrie Suite without my pink pyjamas and my four-wheeled friend, the trolley. Odd, too, to be legitimately parking myself on the sofa. Even though I didn't quite dare put my feet up, just taking the weight off them was a blessing. Wearing 'temporary acting manager' smart heels was taking its toll after months of being in trainers most of the day. Manager of the hotel is a very upright position involving a surprising number of hours walking or standing but rarely sitting, and so I was glad to seize this opportunity.

I remembered coming into the Valkyrie Suite after Mr Clark's post-launch drinks party and finding the fag stub and pâté hedgehog, which I remembered now as the ultimate symbol of my degradation. How downtrodden and insignificant I had felt, trailing my 'to-such-depths-have-I-sunk' despair behind me with the vacuum cleaner. I thought of Chrissie, our new member of housekeeping, who would be in here tomorrow clearing up our mess, and hoped she wouldn't feel the same. At least she wouldn't have a Poliakov shooting ice needles at her heart. I hoped she'd find me a fairer boss. My mornings on my knees cleaning toilets had taught me more about the importance of feeling your work is noticed and valued than sitting behind a desk at Grearson's ever could. I was determined no member of my staff – temporary and acting though I was – should feel that his or her work was overlooked by management. In fact, my two months cleaning the Valkyrie Suite and other Wagnerian extremities had provided me with so many challenges to my understanding of myself that, even now, in my comparatively elevated situation, I still felt unsettled and unbalanced. Another good reason to park myself on the sofa and contemplate the change.

My sit-down was cut short. Mrs A arrived in a vibrant purple-and turquoise-print kaftan, and I had to struggle to my feet to greet her and tell her how gorgeous she looked. It was her first time in the Valkyrie Suite, and she looked it over professionally, comparing it with the guest suites on her round. Dave cleaned up well too, and had put on a smart white shirt and navy-striped tie. He stood around looking uncomfortable without his clipboard, but as soon as Matt arrived the two of them got stuck into a deep analysis of City's problems in attack and defence. They seemed to communicate well despite speaking such extreme versions of the same language. We were a strange mixture of guests with few communal topics of conversation apart from Poliakov, and we quickly chewed that one up. There had been reports that he'd been seen in London, but nothing definite. We all heartily wished he would be brought to face justice. Mrs A and Moira then discovered a mutual fascination with herbal medicine, and Sheila tackled Marc one more time about Gavin Strutt. Phil and I were left to chat about Sheila.

"She's a terrier – never lets a thing go once she's sunk her teeth into it. But then you know," said Phil.

"You still haven't told her, have you?" I asked.

"Timing's important," he said. "It's never quite been right. You know how she gets before a production. Then there's been all this excitement." Before I could chivvy him, Marc called for silence. He felt the need to make another speech.

"Frustrated actor," mumbled Phil. He thanked Phil, Sheila, Matt and Moira for their help and their discretion. He apologised once more to Mrs A, Dave, myself and the rest of the staff for having inflicted Poliakov on us, and praised once again our vigilance, intelligence and courage. He added:

"You have my assurance that I will personally vet the

candidates for the manager's job and make a permanent appointment before I return to London."

"But," Mrs A objected, "manager is Miss Pru."

"Miss Baxter, Prudence, is doing an excellent job as temporary, acting manager," Marc agreed, "and she will of course be interviewed for the post."

"What do you mean 'interviewed' – you know her," Sheila said. "You'd be mad to consider appointing anyone else." Sheila had been at the cocktails and the little self-censorship she exercised when sober deserted her completely after a tequila sunrise or three.

"We want to be fair to everyone," Marc tried to placate her. "We need to think about the future development of the hotel. There are some very experienced applicants who've worked in hotel management in all parts of the world."

"We? I hope you're not going to let Gavin in on this decision," Phil joked.

"But Pru has come up with capital ideas for the hotel," Matt championed. "She's suggested this splendid initiative with the Richard III Society – lectures and dedicated weekends and such."

"And there's the thing we said we'd help out with – the Local History Society and the Lit and Phil Society getting together to do a presentation on the history of the building," added Moira. "BBC Radio Leicester's going to cover it."

"And don't forget the RATS," Sheila intervened. "We've agreed we'll offer murder-mystery dinners or even weekends. They've been very popular when we've done them before. They will grab the punters. But if you bring in new blood I'm not sure we'll be able to offer you the same deal. Pru's a friend." Sheila draped an arm over my shoulder and gazed at me as if I were being transported in the morning.

Since the others had blown my trumpet, I remained silent. I knew that the job of manager had been advertised. I'd written the advert and sifted the replies, but I had sincerely thought we were just complying with the labour laws by advertising. Although I had insisted on my temporary, acting status in everything I'd said or written, it had never really occurred to me that, when the time came for those qualifiers to be removed, I would be stepping down the ladder and not up to full-time manager. I had thought, but saw now that I had been wrong to rely on this, that Marc had all but promised me the job – a reward to me, or a salve to his conscience for Poliakov's attacks.

Marc directed a smile at me and repeated his assurance that I was a strong candidate for the post if my experience of the last eight days hadn't already put me off. I made a point of not returning his smile and he changed the subject.

"I was very pleased to receive your invitation to the charity premiere of the RATS production on Saturday," he said to Phil and Sheila. "I'd like to come if I can."

"It's an exciting week," said Phil. "Dress is tomorrow."

"And yes, he will be wearing one," Sheila interrupted and giggled. Phil's smile looked more like a touch of indigestion.

"Then we open on Wednesday," he continued, "with the charity premiere in aid of the local hospice."

"And I had that brilliant idea to spice up the premiere and make lots of money for the hospice," Sheila said. "Put it out on local radio last weekend, thanks to Uncle Matt, and it's already stirred things up." Dramatic pause to grab the attention of the few who weren't yet in the know. "I've challenged the male members of the audience to come in drag. They have to pay a small dress fee-"

"Which is doubled if they wear a large dress," Matt interrupted. Sheila glared at him then got the joke and began to laugh.

"No, they pay double if they turn up in trousers," she laughed. "Prize for the best costume."

"I think it's a bit bizarre myself," Matt commented. "What do you say, Dave, would you go to the theatre dressed as a woman?"

"Ya wot? Ya mean inna frock?" Dave seemed to think his leg was being pulled.

"We're doing *Charley's Aunt*. Do you know it?" asked Phil. Dave looked blank. "Well in the play one of the chaps – that's me – dresses up as the aunt of one of the other chaps."

"Wot, like in panto?" Dave asked.

"Something like that," Phil agreed.

"Giz me the creeps, men in frocks," said Dave, "though Dame Edna's a good laff. Won't catch me doing it though."

"You don't know what you're missing, Dave, does he Phil?" asked Sheila. "Phil's really enjoyed the dressing up. He makes a lovely woman." Phil tried a smile but looked instead as if that touch of indigestion had become full-scale heartburn.

"Come on, Dave man. Let's you and me go," urged Mrs A. "I lend you me kaftan and some beads. You make a fine woman." She went off into one of her infectious cackles. I noticed that Marc was smiling at the banter, but staring straight at me.

At the end of the evening, he asked me, as he showed the others out, if I wouldn't mind staying a few more minutes to 'talk business'.

"Play the sympathy card," Sheila stage-whispered as she passed me. But I knew better than she did what was on Mr Clark's mind.

"Have another drink, Prudence. I'll call you a taxi." He didn't wait for my reply, but went straight over to pour us both a brandy.

"Not for me, I've had enough already. And I'm fine going home on the bus. Could I just have some water?" He poured a glass of water without replying and then, right on cue, came the upward, searching look as he handed me the drink and the question.

"This idea of Sheila's – the dressing up – does it come from you?"

"I knew you'd think that. No it does not. I keep my promises, unlike some people." Mouth was taking over the function of brain this evening.

"Meaning that I don't?" There it was: I'd pushed the right button. "What exactly do you imagine I've promised you?"

"Well, I did think I'd been promised this job."

"You have the job."

"But only acting and temporary – until the end of the month. Until someone better comes along. I'm just a stopgap. Compared to Ivan, I'm wonderful, but compared to a thirty-five-year-old-with-experience-in-multi-national-chain, I'm rubbish."

"Your words, not mine."

"So next month I have to go back to being office manager. Or should I sack Chrissie and start cleaning suites again?" This wasn't the direction I'd wanted this conversation to go in, but I found that although I thought I'd taken control, the conversation was driving me. Fizzy wine always makes me froth up like this. I should never touch the stuff.

"Which would you prefer?" He seemed to be enjoying this, which fed my anger.

"Neither. As a matter of fact I'd rather go back to haunting the Jobless Centre than work for someone who doesn't trust me."

"Quite right too, good for you. So who is it who doesn't trust you?"

"You know perfectly well I'm talking about you, you idiot." He was deliberately provoking me now. He considered my outburst, then put his glass down and began counting on his fingers.

"I've trusted you with the management of my hotel – sorry," he paused as I was about to intervene to correct himself, "the temporary, acting management of this hotel. I've trusted you to draw up a shortlist of candidates for manager, with your name at the top of the list. I've trusted you with knowledge about my personal life that could be detrimental to my career if made public. So, in the face of all that evidence I have some difficulty, I must admit it, in understanding why you think I don't trust you."

"But you accused me just now of having told Sheila your secret." He picked up his glass and drank a mouthful of brandy. Then I got the direct look to camera.

"I thought, I wondered, if you hadn't suggested the idea to Sheila as a way of helping me."

"Helping you?"

"Giving me a legitimate excuse to do something I've always wanted to do, but never had the guts to go through with: go out in public as a woman." There was a convoluted logic to that suggestion that pleased me, and I wished I had thought of it. Could I still get away with claiming that the thought had crossed my mind, but I'd been too cautious to follow it through? No, he'd seen the dawn of enlightenment glow on my face. Not fast enough at thinking on your feet these days, Pru.

"I said nothing to Sheila," I reassured him. "But I do think that's a brilliant idea. I think you should go. It's in support of a local charity and so it'll be great publicity for you and the hotel. And what's more, I'll come with you, if you like. I mean I have to be there anyway, but I'll support you, help you prepare."

"I don't know," he said. "It could all very easily backfire. Local press is sure to be there. Someone might get the wrong idea." He was weighing the options, but I thought he might well come down on the side of taking the risk. He just needed time to be reconciled to the idea. True, it was his idea, but it had taken him by surprise and still seemed a bit daring to him. It was pointless to push him.

"I'm sorry I lost my temper just now," I said. "I am grateful, really." I picked up my things to leave.

"You know what I think?" he said at the door. "One of us has a problem with trust. And even after meeting all those villains in nine series of *The Truth*, it's not me."

# Chapter Thirty-five

I made the appointment with the personal shopper at Debenhams for three o'clock. Marc was waiting for me at the entrance to the store. He had been cornered by two elderly ladies. They apparently expected him to catch the so-called graffiti artist who had vandalised their local bus stop. Since he wasn't able to transform himself into Superman – there being no suitable phone booth in the neighbourhood – he had promised to speak to the local council about repairs. I could see that he needed rescuing before he could make a rash promise to build them a new bus shelter and fill it full of cut flowers.

"I'm very sorry, ladies, but I must take Mr Clark away now. He has a very pressing appointment at three o'clock. We have just four minutes to get there and Mr Clark hates unpunctuality."

"Don't let us keep you, luv," said the lady with the grey beret.

"You won't forget, will you me duck? Fairview Lane bus stop. It's an eyesore and the wind whistles through it!" said her friend with the tartan shopper.

In Ladies Fashion, our personal shopper was waiting for us with a professional smile that turned to astonishment. She began to gush:

"You're Marc Clark, aren't you? This is exciting. I'd no idea it was you. In my appointment book it just says Baxter. I've never met anyone famous before." The professional veneer was very thin. One face from TV and she was flustered and forgot to ask us to sit down. I sat on the couch anyway and gave my temporary-acting-managerial feet their afternoon treat. She went on. "I love your programme. It's the one thing on TV my partner and I don't fight over. I think you're very brave tackling all those horrible people. Jason, my partner, says he wouldn't fancy meeting some of the characters you talk back to, and he's into martial arts."

Marc, when he could get a word in, thanked her, gave her a warm smile and reminded her that a whole team of people made the programme. He was just the frontman. But she repeated how brave she thought him, and what an interesting programme it was, and how she never missed it, and only then spotted me.

"Oh, I am sorry. In the appointment diary it's written 'a selection of evening wear in plus sizes'. The selection I've made will be too large for this lady." As Marc kept silent, she had to deal with me.

"The selection is actually for Mr Clark, odd as that may seem. You see, he has been invited to the charity premiere of the new production by the Ratae Amateur Theatre Society of *Charley's Aunt*. The director has challenged all the male members of the audience to dress in drag – because of the theme of the play. Mr Clark of course is never one to turn down a challenge and he doesn't want to seem too stuck-up."

"So, it's another daring assignment for you?" laughed the assistant, still ignoring me. I could almost see her fingers twitching to Tweet this story to her Twitter coven, as she twinkled at him.

"Unfortunately, Mr Clark's female acquaintances can't help him out by lending him something because of the large size he requires." That wasn't strictly true. Some of Sheila's clothes would have fitted him, but he had baulked at asking her. "But he would like something feminine and not too Widow Twanky."

"Oh I've picked some beautiful things. You'd be amazed at the range we have now. Plus sizes are starting to get less frumpy. But – I hope you don't mind me making the suggestion – wouldn't it be cheaper to hire something, if it's just for one occasion?" she helpfully suggested.

"That might still be an option, depending on what you have to offer. Mr Clark is rather pressed for time," I urged. "Could we just see your selection?"

The personal shopper service has its own dedicated changing room, which is why I had chosen it. Marc could hardly try clothes on in a women's changing room. Left to his own devices he would have worn a chiffon thing from his own wardrobe, in Mondrian blocks of colour. I didn't even need to see it on him to be able to tell him it would make him look like a walking advert for the Tate Modern café. He was cut by the criticism, but quickly placated by the offer of this appointment in order to try on lots of new clothes with the benefit of professional advice.

He played his role well. I was reminded of Phil's observation about Marc being a thwarted actor. He pretended to be embarrassed at being in a 'women's area' of the store, he gave the appearance of not knowing how to get the clothes on, struggling with zips and thrusting his arms awkwardly into sleeves. He feigned indifference to the colours and fabrics, the diamanté, sequins and embroidery. He laughed at his image in the mirror and attempted a catwalk sashay to make the assistant laugh. He clutched at both our hands to haul himself up onto the one pair of high heels she could find in his size. In fact, he made the whole forty-minute display of 'testosterone gamely thrusting its way into feminine weeds' so amusing for our assistant, that I was surprised someone didn't call the manager and have us all sectioned.

Yet whenever he saw that the assistant was distracted, he chanced a longer look in the mirror; a few seconds' concentrated appraisal of the creature who stared back at him. And from time to time his hand would run gently over the cloth as if to smooth a wrinkle. He caught me once watching the private moment and gave me a smile of real pleasure and shy gratitude.

We, that is the personal shopper and I, for Marc wouldn't allow himself to express an opinion, finally settled on an amber silk dress and jacket with appliqué and seed pearl embroidery. To me it was obvious that Marc's personal selection had been the pink chiffon, one-shouldered creation with diamanté trim. He kept looking back longingly to where it lay discarded on the chair, whilst the assistant began to pack his purchases.

"Walking pink blancmange," I confided to him. "Even worse than me in the Bijou uniform you chose."

"Is that a subtle hint that I have no taste?" he asked.

"You should know by now that I don't do subtle. You have terrible taste."

The assistant laughed:

"I think the lady has made an excellent choice, Mr Clark. It's a very elegant outfit and it does match your colouring."

"If you're ganging up on me then I've no hope. Just have to accept defeat and liberate the credit card." She laughed again and led the way to the cash desk:

"In my experience very few men know what suits them. But in this case you've got an excuse. I mean you've never bought a dress for yourself before, have you?"

On Wednesday, the night of the premiere, I rang the bell of the Valkyrie Suite at 6.30. We'd arranged that I would arrive early to advise on accessories, make-up and wig. I didn't want my handiwork in selecting the perfect outfit to be undone by an injudicious application of powder-blue eyeshadow or the wearing of a Dolly Parton wig. The bedroom, when Marc showed me in there, looked like an explosion in an Accessorize warehouse with his entire collection of wigs, costume jewellery and make-up decorating every surface.

"I love the style of this dress and the material, but don't you think it makes me look a little matronly?"

"I hate to tell you this," – a figure of speech, of course because we're really bursting to tell the other person – "but you're not twenty-three any more. You will look timelessly elegant," I reassured. "You don't want to look like one of those sad women who get stuck in a fashion rut from their teenage years and never grow up. Nor the even sadder ones who just copy the latest fashion, however inappropriate to their age and size." I shuddered at the memory of tweed shorts and aubergine tights on the stubby little legs of a woman who catches my bus.

There were some protests when I vetoed the violet eyeshadow and blue mascara, and he did keep trying on the blonde wig, vainly hoping to win my approval. But the end result of my labours transfixed him. A matte foundation, a dark blusher, eyeshadow in shades of brown and beige, a little dark red lipstick and a final dusting with a touch of shimmer powder, the medium-length mousy-brown wig, and he looked a handsome, rather strong-featured woman: Katherine Hepburn meets Bette Davies. But he looked like a woman, not a man in drag. He wasn't disturbing like Phil in drag, but solid: a woman you'd approach in the street to ask directions. As long as he didn't walk, or talk, other women would accept him as one of their own.

"This is me," he said. "The way I often feel I could be." Then he ruined the image in the mirror by swallowing hard and letting that very masculine Adam's apple rise and fall in his throat.

"Don't you dare start shedding womanly tears," I said, only half joking, "or we'll be another hour redoing your eyes."

"Thank you, Pru," he said, never taking his eyes off the face in the glass. "I can't tell you how I feel. Transformed, liberated, quite like Stephanie."

"Who's Stephanie?"

"My alter ego. The woman I like to turn into sometimes and forget I've been lumbered with the body of a rugby league player on steroids."

"You seem more of an Anna to me. Or a Deborah, or even a Jocelyn. Yes, I think I quite like Jocelyn for you."

When I could finally unstick him from the mirror, I offered to drive us. We could have walked across town from the Bijou, but neither of us fancied dragging our finery through the city centre on a weekday night. He approved of the solidity of my battered old Volvo.

“You know Pru,” he told me as I drove, “sitting here, I feel like Boudicca heading into battle.”

“It is a bit of a chariot,” I agreed. “Other people stay out of my way.”

“Yes, that’s true. But it was more the way you drive as if you’re cutting down the Roman legions that made me think of it,” he said.

# Chapter Thirty-six

I was lying in bed trying to sleep. Tomorrow the interviews would be taking place. I was dreading meeting all the other candidates. I needed my sleep. I wanted to make a good impression on Gavin Strutt, the co-owner, who was gracing us with his presence for the interviews. If I turned up with bags under my eyes large enough to hold several auto-parts from his yard, he wouldn't necessarily think I was a good front woman for his hotel.

A weird sound woke me up. It was like a very large sofa cushion deflating, as if someone had recorded that sound and amplified it. What could it be? As a back note to the sound there was something else. A human cry, a scream? It was over in seconds and the silence, or at least the normal night sounds of the house, returned. I switched on the lamp. My alarm clock showed me it was 3.30. I got up and put on the light. I crossed to the door and opened it a little. There were no lights showing, no torch beam. Everything was normal. Curiosity pushed me on. I switched on the landing light and went downstairs to the kitchen. I checked all the doors and windows. Everything was as I had left it. Finally I went into the ground floor room of the tower and there on the floor saw the source of the noise. White dust, which I had stirred into a tiny whirlwind by opening the door, was beginning to settle again. The ceiling of the room had finally caved in and was strewn in heaps across the floor. As I looked at the devastation, I saw one of the heaps was moving, making muffled groans. It was a human form, dusted white like a piece of fish waiting to be battered and fried. There was a dark stain spreading from the head end and I made out a hand. It was clasping a mobile phone that still glowed with life. Unafraid, I knelt down to see who my unfortunate intruder might be and as my face drew near to the dust-covered head, the eyelids snapped open. I was gazing into the dead eyes of Poliakov.

My alarm woke me. It was 6.30 and I wondered how I could have gone back to bed and left Poliakov lying downstairs dead. I had to go downstairs to the ground floor room of the tower and look inside to see what had happened. Nothing had happened. The dusty floor was empty of body or debris, and the water-stained ceiling was still holding – just. Poliakov had never been there except as part of my nightmare. My brain felt like the wadding in a cuddly toy and I had to rush to get ready for work and the interview.

On the local radio, as I was driving to work, they reported that there had been a shooting incident overnight in Nottingham. A man was in hospital and two others were being questioned. 'Well,' I thought, 'that's Nottingham. It's becoming a real Wild West frontier town these days. Thank God I don't live there.' But as soon as I arrived at the hotel, Sharifa, one of the English-speaking receptionists that I had appointed, told me the news.

"Mr Clark asked me to tell you he got a message this morning that the police had found, let me see the name… "

"Poliakov," I supplied. "Where?"

"Nottingham. They were called to a shooting incident and this man, Poliakov, was taken to hospital. They didn't say if it was serious or not. Is he a friend of yours?" I filled her in on the details of the story. I hadn't known until that moment how much Ivan's continued freedom had been playing on my mind. He'd been really close in Nottingham. Now he was caught I could begin to relax and stop looking over my shoulder. It was unkind of me, perhaps, but for all that he'd done to those poor people, and for the fear he'd put into me, I made a silent wish that he'd been shot somewhere that really hurt.

*

In the foyer, on a display board, we have the double-page spread from the *Mercury*'s feature on the charity premiere. It's been a talking point for the managerial candidates all morning. The feature shows Marc, resplendent in amber, tripping down the plush red carpet Sheila had dug out for the male guests to walk along – à la film premiere. In the pictures you can see him playing Stephanie the starlet. There are photos of him with other guests in drag, with the cast, with Phil as Donna Lucia, and one with Sheila and Phil. That one with Sheila beaming between the two of them in drag makes me particularly uncomfortable. There's a picture of him being presented with a bottle of champagne, which he later gave to the cast, as his first prize for Drag Queen of the evening. There are quotes from his East Midlands TV interview, quotes from his local radio slot, and pictures of him autographing programmes for fans. The full review of the play, which Mr Clark had pronounced 'most enjoyable', was relegated to a later page. Still, it was all good publicity for the drama group and the hotel, and made a good few thousand for the hospice.

It's also proved a useful little test for the would-be managers. How they reacted to this display of their prospective boss in prize-winning drag, and the conclusions drawn about them from their comments, were passed on to me by Mrs A and Sharifa, our new receptionist. Their hot tip was a young Australian called Ethan, who'd laughed at the photos and said how cool it would be to work for a guy who could let his hair down and wasn't just a stuffed shirt. He'd also recognised Mrs A in one of the photos in her Nigerian dress, and they'd had a long chat about his girlfriend who was from Kano and worked as an accountant.

I had to admit he was the least irritating of the bunch, and the only one who didn't either dismiss me or become icy, when I was introduced as the acting manager. He'd moved around quite a lot, but had glowing references from all his employers, apparently. I had made sure to follow up all the references, sending them on to Marc and Mr Strutt. We couldn't risk employing another Ivan.

My turn for interview came in the afternoon. I was the last to go in and couldn't decide whether they were saving the best till last, or were just slotting me in to keep me quiet. I had met Gavin Strutt first thing in the morning and hadn't taken to him. I couldn't get past the story of how he'd made his money in scrap metal. I had an instant snapshot of him as the sort of Steptoe character who used to drive first a horse and cart, and then a pick-up lorry, through the streets collecting scrap, when I was growing up. I had the same feeling I'd had all those years ago about the 'rag-and-bone man'. Gavin Strutt was just such a man who'd con me out of my gran's valuable old, brass bedstead in exchange for a striped lollipop and a packet of balloons.

We didn't get off to the best of starts.

"Firstly," said Mr Strutt, "I'd like to thank you for your presence of mind and your personal courage in helping to solve the problems we had with your predecessor." His smile was calculated to be ingratiating, but I wasn't going to be smarmed. This was the man who'd appointed Poliakov.

"Problems that wouldn't have existed if you… if the proper recruitment procedure had been followed. As it was, the low-paid staff were made to jump through hoops by Smart People, whilst the manager was shooed in by you."

"Quite." He looked like a man who wasn't used to failing in his charm offensive. I'd got him ruffled. "I had heard that you speak your mind, and it's very refreshing to meet someone who doesn't mince words. In fact I've heard a lot about you from my business partner, and from the staff. But of course, I'd like to hear from you. Tell me something about yourself."

My replies to this and subsequent questions sounded defiant, even to my ears. It wasn't the tone I'd wanted to adopt. I'd planned to be quietly confident, and detached. After all this was a man who was probably prepared to settle for the easiest option, as he'd done with Poliakov, and just make my post permanent. So why was I speaking to him as if he owed me something? Well, because I found sitting there that I felt he did owe me something. He was responsible for the fact that I'd been appointed a chambermaid and not manager. He was responsible for the misery of those months of changing duvet covers and inhaling antibacterial spray. Above all he was responsible for unleashing Ivan in all his nastiness: the slashed tyres, the attack in the car park. A simple 'thank you for your help' wasn't going to be enough.

Marc intervened to ask me what personal qualities I'd bring to the job. I reeled off my list, daring either of them to challenge me. Mr Strutt attempted a professional skills question:

"What would you do as manager if you believed a member of the staff were stealing from the hotel?" A standard question but an unfortunate one. I glowered at Marc.

"I didn't steal. That whole episode was set up by Poliakov to get me dismissed. He had to prevent me from working in the office."

"Miss Baxter, I'm not referring to any incident. My question is hypothetical. I want to know what you'd do as manager." I calmed myself and trotted out the correct response learned off by heart from a management handbook, but in a way that let him know what a pathetic question I thought it was if he wanted to gain information about someone's abilities. After all it could be answered correctly by a trained parrot if its owner had read the manual.

They brought the interview to a close in the usual way by asking me if I had any questions.

"I believe I know the hotel well enough. My only question is about the speed with which you'll reach a decision on the appointment." They told me I'd know by tomorrow at the latest. I don't know who was most relieved at the end of the sparring match. I can't tell you what they did after I left the room, but I told Sharifa I was not to be disturbed, went into the office, swallowed a couple of aspirin and sat looking gloomily at the wall.

# Chapter Thirty-seven

The phone on my desk, ringing just before six, puzzled me. For a moment I had no idea where I was.

"Pru?" Marc's voice. "I thought you'd be home by now, I phoned there first. Gavin and I would like you to have dinner with us. It has to be an early meal because he's got to drive back to London this evening. See you in the bar in ten minutes." He put the phone down. Refusal was not an option, then.

"Join us in a glass of Prosecco, Miss Baxter," Gavin Strutt called as I entered the bar.

"Surely there's not room for three of us in one glass, is there?" I said. Mr Strutt looked puzzled and then gave a huge shout of laughter.

"Marc said you had a sense of humour," he said, "well hidden." Lesley, the waitress, produced another glass, lifted the bottle from its cooler and poured. As she handed me the glass, she winked. She thought the manager's job was in the bag too. Fizzy wine and I don't mix, I know, but I accepted the glass, for this was a celebration.

"I think we've all earned this," said Marc. "Certainly you haven't worked this hard in years, have you, Gavin? Cheers!"

"Can we have the menus too, love?" Mr Strutt called to Lesley who came running. "Sorry we have to eat in a rush like this," he apologised to me, "but I have to get back tonight."

"Should you be drinking, then," I asked, "if you have to drive back?"

"I pay my driver not to drink," he said, regarding me levelly. "And it seems I pay you to sharpen up in the knife box. Can we call a truce?"

"Relax, Pru," Marc urged. "The interview's over."

"I thought you had curries and such here," said Mr Strutt, glancing at the menu.

"Only on Sundays and Wednesdays now," I told him. I explained to him how Smart People had appointed two head chefs. I had had to intervene before they could carve each other into steak tartare. Sanjay had said he could earn more money and have some evenings free if he went to work with his cousin in freelance catering. So that had left Giorgio as head chef, cooking the Italian menu. But I had persuaded Sanjay to come and do all-day tiffin on Sundays, Giorgio's day off, and an Indian regional menu on Wednesdays. "Now that Giorgio's boss of the kitchen, he's much more amenable – even learning to make puri and samosas."

"You see how resourceful she is?" Marc commented.

"That's exactly the word Chris Grearson used; resourceful," said Mr Strutt. "He also said you used to put the fear of God into the shop-floor workers – which I can well imagine. Said he couldn't have managed them without you."

"That was sweet of him." I was genuinely touched by his tribute to my capacity to terrorize.

"I wasn't just being polite when I said earlier that I liked plain speaking," Mr Strutt went on. "Marc will back me up on this: when people see you've got some cash, when they see you've got clout, they become 'yes men' – brown-nosers. You get to the point where you just want to hear someone tell you his honest opinion. I like that about you, Miss Baxter." He drank his wine. "I can't bring myself to call you Pru, like Marc does, even if you'd let me, which you probably wouldn't." He signalled to Lesley and she came to take our orders.

"I like your honesty," he went on, "your 'can-do' attitude, your loyalty to your boss – thirty years at Grearson's wasn't it? You hardly look old enough." I huffed at that exaggerated piece of flattery and he laughed. "All right, all right. I'll put the flannel away and stick to the point." He topped up all our glasses. Ready for a toast? "Point one is," he continued, "you've done a great job as acting manager, and you could obviously run the Bijou with your eyes closed. Point two is that you alerted Marc to the people-smuggling and we're both very grateful for the fact that you headed off a real 'shit hits the fan' scandal." I was drinking in all this praise with the fizzy wine and nearly missed the next bit. "But, the final point is we think the Bijou needs a fresh start. We've offered the job to Ethan Collins and he's accepted it."

"Gavin," Marc tried to interrupt, "that's not quite–"

"No. We agreed I'd do the talking," he went on.

"I think you've already said enough," I said and stood up to leave. I wanted to go whilst I could do so with dignity. The slap of that rejection had numbed me. Going through my head was,

'Thanks for holding things together, thanks for saving our bacon, now, piss off!'

"Please sit down, Miss Baxter, and let me finish."

"All I need to know," I said, fighting to keep my voice low and calm, "is what notice you require me to serve."

"You'll start the handover next week," Gavin Strutt continued, "but I wish you'd let me finish."

"Next week? I see. Fine. Thank you gentlemen. Enjoy your–"

"For God's sake sit down, Pru," Marc snapped, "and do as you're told for once."

I had sat down before I was aware of it. Good thing I had been sitting on the sofa. I might have missed a chair. No one had ever spoken to me in that tone, not even my father. I was gathering myself up again to tell them so when Mr Strutt started up again.

"All your previous experience is as a personal assistant-"

"I assure you, you don't need to justify your choice to me," I interrupted. The upper lip had never been so stiff, but I had to get in quickly. I wasn't sure how much longer the glue would hold.

"Justify be buggered," Mr Strutt boomed. "I'm trying to offer you a bloody job, but you won't let me get a bloody word in bloody edgeways." Offer me a bloody job? What was he talking about? Hadn't he just told me he'd given the job to the Australian? Was he going to ask me if I would be prepared to work as Ethan's assistant? I was confused.

"Well, go on," I conceded.

"You have no family, no ties here, that's right, isn't it? I know about your house. Marc mentioned it, but I mean you could easily move somewhere else, couldn't you; abroad for example?"

"Well, yes, I suppose so." I'd never thought of moving. I wasn't sure how I felt about the idea, it being so novel. Was he suggesting I go on a gap year?

"I've got a project I've just started up in Croatia, near Porec

– a little holiday village, apartments, cottages, restaurant, water sports, you know the sort of thing. It's just ready to open, all the staff in place. They know what to do. They can run it. What I need is someone like you, mature, resourceful, trustworthy, to keep an eye on it for me. Represent me, as it were. Stop the fiddles before they start. Keep the buggers up to scratch."

"But I don't speak Croatian." It was the first objection that came into my head. He laughed:

"Who does? The staff all speak English, and most of the punters will be English or German or Scandinavian. Language is no problem." I was silent, trying to imagine myself in another country, in another job. Impossible. I'd only ever been to Spain and Italy on package tours. I couldn't create the picture. We were called through to the restaurant and our food was served, which delayed my answer. I discovered that eating barely slowed down Mr Strutt's rate of chatter.

"Of course, it's seasonal work, March to October, couple of weeks over Christmas and New Year, but I'd pay you an annual salary – bit more than you'd get here, plus an apartment there. I can easily find you other things to do in the off-season: lots of projects I don't get time for, that would benefit from a visitation. Lots of travelling, of course, but I'm sure you'd enjoy that." He paused for breath. "So what do you think?" I didn't know what I thought, would have been the truth. My chance to travel – here it was, together with real responsibility. Someone at last appreciated my qualities. And wasn't he right? Wouldn't I be brilliant at 'keeping the buggers up to scratch'? But before I could answer, his phone rang and he glanced at it, excused himself and went out to start up the same rapid patter with the person on the line.

"It's a bit of a shock," I confessed to Marc.

"Gavin's always been something of a whirlwind," he smiled. "He's taken to you, though. He's what you might call a 'rough diamond' but if he likes you, and you don't let him down – which I know you never would – he's a good man to work for."

"He's a bit full of himself," I said. "I'm not sure that I like that." Lesley came to clear the starters.

"Is everything all right for you?" she asked.

"Very good indeed," Marc assured her with a smile. When she'd gone he said, "I hope you're not too disappointed about the job at the Bijou?"

"I do like the job," I considered. "Yes, I am. I think I am disappointed. That's why I can't think. Can't take in what he's asking me." Mr Strutt returned to the table.

"Sorry about that. The damned thing's always going off. Now, where was I?"

"I think you should tell Pru about your other little project that concerns her," Marc reminded him.

"Ah yes, your house. Must be a worry for you. I mean you couldn't rent it out the state it's in, if you fly off to Croatia."

"When did you see my house?" I asked.

"Marc showed me it on Google Earth. It's in a sorry state. I remember seeing it when I was a lad – house with a tower in the snobby part of town. I always wondered where the other towers had gone. I thought it was a ruined castle." He laughed.

"It's Edwardian," I told him.

"I never was much good at history or anything else at school, except for answering back," he confessed. Lesley brought the main course and Marc poured the wine. "This looks good," said Mr. Strutt, and attacked his osso buco with relish. But he still kept up the chatter about my house. "It's too small for a student hostel, which is a shame as it's so close to the uni. There's already a lot of unused office space in that area, so I wouldn't convert it to business use. Mmm, this is good." He was silent for a moment, chewing. "Your best bet is warden-controlled accommodation for the over-sixties. With an extension on the back you'd get ten, twelve units in there and still have space for a bit of garden and a car park. Good area, a few local shops, close to Viki Park, close to bus routes. Good doctors I suppose? Premium prices – and it's the over-sixties who've got the money."

A whirlwind was right. I told him:

"Mr Strutt, I don't have the means to repair the roof, let alone convert it into a senior citizens' fun park."

"Obviously not. I'd do the building," he said, dredging through the sauce on his plate with a piece of bread. "You sell the property to me, your worries are over. Get yourself something smaller. Or you could have one of the apartments – book the one in the tower if you like."

"But I don't want to sell my house," I protested. "And I'm not over sixty."

"You'll have squatters in it if you leave it in that state and go off to Croatia."

"But I'm not going off to Croatia. I haven't accepted your job." Careful, Pru. Keep brain in control of mouth. Do not burn any boats here. "I need time to think about it. It would be a huge change for me. I can't make such an important decision just like that. You'll have to give me more time to think about both your suggestions." Good girl.

# Chapter Thirty-eight

It was a relief when Gavin Strutt had shaken hands all round, left compliments for the chef, a healthy tip for Lesley, and disappeared into the night.

"You look tired, Pru," Marc commented.

"Tired? I feel as if I've been run over by a giant loudspeaker on caterpillar tracks. Is he always so relentless?"

"Pretty much so," he laughed. "Let's finish the wine in my suite. After all, Gavin's paid for it." This time I did put my feet up on the sofa in the Valkyrie Suite – asked no permission and gave no apologies.

"He was probably even more full-on than usual today because he's embarrassed about Poliakov. He could have sustained quite a lot of damage to his reputation if the press had got hold of it first. And it was a relief to both of us this morning to hear that the police had finally picked Poliakov up. I honestly thought he would have skipped the country by now." He settled into the armchair after having refreshed our glasses. "It's not like Gavin to make a mistake."

"How did he come to make this one? He was rather shy of talking about it – about the only subject he was reticent on."

"From what I can make out, he was paying back a favour to a business friend, who is no longer a friend, and no longer in business. It seems the guy was in serious debt and prepared to swim with the sharks to try and get out of it. He promised those sharks he'd find an opening for them here in the East Midlands and duped Gavin into taking on Poliakov as a favour to him."

"Does he know many murky people, Gavin?" I asked.

"I've never really asked him. I think people who are successful in business have to be prepared to get into bed with all sorts. But I'd say, as wheeler-dealers go, he's pretty honest." Mr Strutt could slide his paunch into bed beside whomever he chose, but working for someone who was only 'pretty honest' didn't strike me as compelling.

"What about the post of Office Manager? Couldn't I stay on and work for this young Australian?" Gavin Strutt's monologue had excluded discussion of this topic too.

"You ask me, Pru, but I think you should be asking yourself. Could you do that?" He gave me a knowing look that I didn't think he had any right to give me on such a short acquaintance.

"Why not? I worked for Mr Grearson for thirty years."

"But you hadn't been the boss at Grearson's before you became his assistant"

"I was never the boss here – only temporary acting," I reminded him. "In any case, whatever you think of me, I'm not a megalomaniac – only when there's an 'r' in the month and the wind's from the north."

"I wouldn't like to be in Ethan's shoes with you as Office Manager," he laughed. I thought about objecting to the suggestion that I'd be the bane of this young man's working life, but I had just to laugh instead, for there was more than a grain of truth in it. I could see myself, lips pursed and arms folded, watching the new manager, mentally intoning, 'that's not the way I would do things,' delighting in every mistake, and undermining every success. Then I suddenly stopped laughing. The vision was too real. I didn't want to become such a bitter ball of envy and spite. There was no possibility of working for young Ethan. Marc was right, damn him. So, the only option I had, apart from the Jobless Centre, was to leave my familiar surroundings and everything I knew, and go off to harass holidaymakers in a latter-day Butlins-by-the-sea, in Croatia. Damn Gavin Strutt too. I had been within spitting distance of taking my rightful place, my desired place as manager of the Bijou, and he had wilfully snatched it away from me for his own selfish ends. It would serve him damned well right if I did go and work for him.

Perhaps I was just tired, but I felt I didn't have the courage to uproot myself and head off into the unknown alone. Those English-speaking foreign personnel would probably see me as Gavin Strutt's Rottweiler – hardly the basis for firm friendships. And even if some of the guests were my age and sympathetic, they would only be there for a fortnight at the most. Who would I talk to? What the hell would I do with myself on my day off? No book club, no RATS. And what would I do with my house? I asked Marc:

"Should I sell my house to Gavin Strutt?"

"You told me it would cost more than you have to restore it. Logically, unless you can get the National Trust to adopt it as a 'time capsule', you'll have to sell it to someone or wait for it to be condemned."

"Might not be such a long wait," I said. Then, "I don't think I'd better have any more of this wine. It's not lifting my mood at all."

"He's got a good track record for sympathetic conversions. After all, he did the Bijou." He smiled at my morose torpor. "I think you'd better sleep on these decisions, Pru. You don't have to rush into anything you don't want to do." My unfocused gaze landed on a photo in a white wooden frame. It was new.

"Is that you, at *Charley's Aunt*?" I asked. He got up and brought the photo over to the sofa. I shuffled my feet out of the way to let him sit down. We examined it together.

"Sheila sent it over. I was very touched. It's rather good, don't you think?" It was a copy of the picture that had appeared in the newspaper – a manically grinning Sheila between the two cross-dressers. The men were undoubtedly more feminine than the woman. But that wasn't the only reason it made me feel uncomfortable. I wasn't quite at home in this 'brave new world' I'd wandered into, however unconscious of it I tried to appear.

"Can you imagine Sheila doesn't know, about Phil? I mean, he hasn't told her."

"Really? I thought she was the ideal supportive partner." He examined her face in the photo. "Sheila's too astute not to know something. Most of us have our own unacknowledged truth that we live with. It's only compromise that lets us get by."

"Yes, that makes sense." Someone else who understood Sheila better than me. "And when is Stephanie's next outing to be?"

He smiled, but in a wistful way I thought. "No. This was a one off." He sighed. "But it was a very special evening."

"What are you talking about? You paid a fortune for that outfit. You have to wear it again. You could get yourself invited to a fancy dress party – or organise one yourself. Now you've set the precedent, you must do it again." He still looked unconvinced. "When we do the Murder Mystery here, you could dress up as a thirties screen siren. That's quite legitimate. Everyone dresses up."

"I doubt if I'll be here then. And nor probably will you. I certainly couldn't be as glamorous as that without my lady's maid to advise me." He fell silent staring at the photo, then said, "I told you that night how liberated I felt, and I enjoyed it to the full because I knew even then it was a sensation I wouldn't be able to repeat." He got up and went to return the photo to its place. Then he turned to face me. "I couldn't have done that without you, Pru. I might have gone along as a man in a dress, but I wouldn't have had the courage to go along as me in a dress. I've tried for years but I've never dared share that part of me with people outside my little group." He laughed. "I never thought when I first saw you in your pink overalls that you'd turn out to have such an effect on me."

I didn't like the way things were going.

"Is this a goodbye speech," I asked, "because if so, you can save your breath and let me get off home. I don't do goodbyes." I tried to ease my feet into my shoes, a necessary preliminary to getting to my feet so that I could declaim my gratitude for past kindness, and walk out of his life, head held high. But I decided hauling myself onto my temporary-acting-manager heels was really an unnecessary conceit. I could declaim just as well sitting down and then shamble out without my shoes. He stayed on his feet however and didn't give me the chance to declaim or shamble.

"I didn't intend to put this to you this evening. I wanted to give you the chance to think about Gavin's offer and not confuse you." At that moment, confusing me further wasn't possible. My brain seemed to have nipped off home and gone to bed leaving my mouth to do the thinking, and I couldn't shape a thought let alone a word. "You've spent all your working life as a PA, as Gavin pointed out. I like to think that we work well together and have developed mutual respect." I nodded. It was so much easier than speaking. "I like the fact that you make me laugh. I even like your bloody-mindedness." I was wrong. I could be more confused. What was this all about? "I suppose what I'm getting at is… Well, might you consider working for me, as a PA? I've never really had one before, just relied on the production team, but now I think I might like it." I waited for more. "I don't know what I could offer you. I'd have to speak to my accountant. I can't even give you a real job description, but we could work something out together, don't you think?" There was still no reaction from me. "I'm sorry," he said, "It sounds like a dodgy deal, doesn't it, but… what do you think?"

Well, of course I didn't think. My brain had gone and wishing for it to come back didn't seem to have any effect. And for once, mouth without brain was remaining silent. I just sat there doing my imitation of a water-spout in a summer drought.

"I knew I should have left it to another time," he said and sat down in the armchair opposite, looking almost as uncomfortable as when I'd caught him dressed in Stephanie's satin slip. "It's just that I thought that if I left it until I next saw you, you would already have snapped up Gavin's offer. I'm going to London tomorrow and back to the States next month." His pause for my reaction was fruitless. "If you could make a decision before then, it would be great to have you on that trip. Natalie would be pleased to see you again. In the long term, you'd probably have to move up to London, at least for a few days a week. And I travel most weeks when we're doing the series. Look," he finished, "think it over. Just sleep on it and-"

"Yes." My mouth finally managed to shape a word.

"... call me with your answer. What?"

"Yes, I'd like to do it," a whole sentence now, albeit a simple one. It was his turn to look blank.

"You will? That's great, Pru." I thought so too. Two job offers in a couple of hours and I'd chosen the right one.

I picked up my shoes and stood up. It didn't matter much if people saw me walking through reception in my stocking feet. Someone else was manager now. I was going to sell my house to Gavin Strutt, move to London as Mr Marc Clark's personal assistant and fly off with him to America. I'd have to get a passport first, of course, but that was a minor administrative matter. There was something much more pressing, a couple of questions that had to be asked before I went downstairs to call a taxi, and end this longest day. I had been heading for the door and my brilliant new future, but stopped:

"There are two things bothering me that I want to raise before I go."

"Ask away." He leaned back comfortably into the armchair.

"First of all, are you obsessed with Wagner?"

"Wagner? No, not that keen on most opera, and especially not Wagner. Why?"

"The Valkyrie Suite." I gestured about me, shoes in hands. He understood and laughed:

"That was Gavin's idea. They're all suites so he wanted to call them something to do with music. He thought the Valkyrie was an especially apt name for my suite. He thinks I'm some kind of 'avenger.'" He laughed. "Now he does like opera. Even sponsors it. I bet you didn't expect that."

"But he was a rag-and-bone man," I couldn't reconcile the two images. He laughed again at that.

"He made his money in scrap metal a long time ago. He's into all types of business now internationally and he's more cultured than you'd think."

"Right," I answered. For he had, indeed, given the right answer to my question. The second one was about something I'd noticed the evening I'd come to the Valkyrie Suite to help him dress for the RATS do. The significance of it was only hitting me now. I hesitated. It was very personal, but I needed an answer.

"Do you wax your legs?"

"What?" The blank look lingered a moment then he laughed and got to his feet.

"You don't want to answer that one, do you?"

"No. I don't mind answering. I'm just trying to work out how the two things are related. I use a razor. I tried a patch test once with wax. I concluded it should be on the UN's list of tortures."

"But you never, ever have hairy legs?"

"No, I can't stand hairy legs." As I finally reached the threshold he opened the door for me and said, "I don't understand, Pru, does all this have some bearing on the job?"

"It might," I answered. "It just might." I turned to give him what I hoped was an enigmatic smile but was probably just a sozzled smirk, and then left, quietly closing the door of the Valkyrie Suite behind me.